LINGER

Edward Fallon

#1

Dying
is a
Wild Night

BRAUN HAUS MEDIA, LLC

This is a work of fiction. All of the characters, organizations, and events portrayed in this novel are either products of the author's imagination or are used fictitiously.

LINGER #1 Dying is a Wild Night
Copyright © 2015 by Braun Haus Media, LLC
All rights reserved.

ISBN-13: 978-0692437070
ISBN-10: 069243707X

Cover design by Braun Haus Media, LLC
Photo Credits:
Serious Boy Portrait © atikinka2/ Dollar Photo Club

The publisher wishes to acknowledge and thank
Robert Gregory Browne
for his contribution to this work

Sign up for the
Braun Haus Media, LLC Newsletter
and get a free ebook.

Yes, that's right.
A free full-length supernatural thriller
from our growing library of books.

See BraunHausMedia.com for details

**Other books in the *Linger* series
available for purchase now**

LINGER

Dying is a Wild Night

PART ONE

"Dying is a wild night and a new road."

~Emily Dickinson

1

Tacoma, Washington
Three Months Ago

BY THE TIME THEY REACHED the house it was already on fire.

The boy had told him this might happen, but they had taken the chance that he was wrong.

He sometimes was.

They sat less than a block away in the man's station wagon, a rapidly declining '64 Rambler Cross Country that was far too old to be on the road. His wife Anna had inherited it from her father, and he in turn from her. There was a time when he had lovingly maintained it for her, but those days were lost—just as Anna was. Part of another life that was as foreign to him now as a goodnight kiss.

As he watched the house burn, he heard the boy rocking quietly on the back seat, where he always sat. With the windows rolled up, the only sound was the creaking of the upholstery and the soft *squeak-squeak* of the springs.

He glanced at the boy in his rearview mirror, looking for any sign that he might be cognizant of the world around him. But that face gave nothing away. The sightless eyes stared at the ceiling as he rocked, his hands clasped together in his lap. He was in the haze, and wherever he'd gone, it didn't look as if he'd be coming back anytime soon.

The man studied the burning house and knew it was a lost cause. There were two fire trucks parked out front, a dozen or more firefighters giving it their best with their hoses, but anyone could see it was well past saving. If this was a crime scene, the fire was probably intentional.

The man wondered—and not for the first time—if the Beast

somehow knew what they were up to and was attempting to cover his tracks. If so, he had underestimated what the boy was capable of, just as the man had, not that many months ago.

To his surprise, the squeak of the springs stopped and the boy was with him again, reaching for the door handle. Back when they first started traveling together, the man would rush to help him, but he had quickly discovered that the blindness was not a handicap. After dealing with this physical limitation for nearly twelve years, the boy was quite capable of helping himself.

He didn't even carry a cane.

The door opened and the smell of smoke and burning wood filled the car as the boy climbed out. It was pointless to ask him any questions. He would communicate when he was ready.

He walked to the front of the car, framed in the windshield as he faced the house. Anyone watching would think that he was just another curious bystander, but the man knew he was doing what he did so well.

The house groaned as chunks of charred wood fell away and crashed to the ground. Then the boy raised a hand, his voice—as always—a melodic presence inside the man's head:

Are you ready?

"Yes," the man said, and reached to the seat beside him for the pencil and sketchpad, flipping to a new blank page as he pulled the pad into his lap.

Then, as the boy sent him the pictures...

...he closed his eyes and began to draw.

2

Santa Flora, California
Today

IF ANYONE WERE TO ASK Detective Lieutenant Kate Messenger how she felt about the prospect of becoming an orphan, she would deny she even thought about it.

She wasn't a child anymore. She was a grown woman and certainly capable of being on her own. She had proven this many years earlier when her mother was killed, a devastating blow that had robbed her of the only parental affection she had ever known.

Her father, always a humorless man, had raised her in the most perfunctory manner possible, making sure she was fed and clothed and housed, but having little to do with the rest of her life.

So, in truth, Kate had been orphaned years ago.

Now, after decades of being subjected to too much beer and far too many cigarettes, Mitchell Messenger's internal organs had finally had enough of him and were rapidly calling it quits. But Kate left questions about the future to others and did only what was expected of her.

Her duty.

Every Sunday and Wednesday night.

.

"I haven't been keeping up with the news," Mitch said, his phlegm-throttled wheeze modulated by the flow of his oxygen tank. "How many bodies did you find?"

He sat in his armchair in a corner of the room as Kate stripped the sheets from his bed. To her surprise, his impending death had turned him into something of a chatterbox, as if he'd decided he needed to make up for all the years of indifferent silence. A former cop himself, he was always asking Kate about the cases she worked—the one thing in their lives they had in common.

She no longer resisted sharing with him. It was the least she could do for a man whose meter was about to run out, even if she didn't particularly like him.

"Six," she said. "Six bodies, if you count the family dog. Mother, father, and three children. All girls."

"Jesus H. Christ. Another fuckin' psycho. They're all over the place these days. You remember Jimmy Jay, don't you?"

"Your ex partner."

"His son's working homicide up in Tacoma now and he tells me they had one just like that a few months ago—family of four. Bastard lit the house on fire trying to make it look like an accident, but they found evidence that the victims' tongues were all cut out."

The old man seemed to relish this detail, as if it had been arranged for his own private amusement. He had no life and nothing to look forward to, but he certainly appeared to take joy in knowing that some people had suffered more than he ever would.

"I remember getting the bulletin on that," Kate said. "And Rusty mentioned it at his retirement party last month. But it's got nothing to do with us."

"Oh? How can you be so sure?"

"The details are off. Completely different M.O. The only real similarity is that an entire family was killed."

"Must be contagious," Mitch grunted. "So what's your play on this one? You gonna call in the Feebs?"

It had been five days since the killings at the Branford house, and with very little in the way of conclusive forensics, Kate was seriously considering such a move. But she wasn't quite ready yet. This was her first big case as head of Major Crimes, and for better or worse, she felt the need to follow it through.

The brutality of the killings certainly pointed to a sick and twisted mind, but whether they were the work of a roving psychopath or simply a ruthlessly brutal tactic to divert attention away from a more personal killing, was a hot topic of debate among the members of her squad.

She wasn't about to debate it with her father, however.

"Hey, did I slur my speech?" he said. "Or do I need a megaphone?"

Kate gathered his sheets into a ball and turned. "No, Mitch, I'm not ready to call in the feds just yet."

"What's the holdup? They've got people with expertise in this area."

"I'm aware of that."

"When I was in the field, I took their help whenever I could. All that territorial bullshit they tell you about in the movies is—"

"I know. I've been doing this for awhile now, remember?"

"Then what's the delay?"

She dumped the ball of sheets on the floor, then crossed to the hallway and opened a linen closet. She always changed his bed when she came here. It gave her something to do other than sit around and stare at him and try to muster up some sympathy where little could be found.

"I'm still working the case," she said. "I want to be sure I haven't missed anything before I throw in the towel."

"So, in other words, you wanna grab the glory." He snorted, a thick, nasally sound that set her teeth on edge. "It's thinking like that lets these assholes get away. Like those gangbangers you let skate last month."

"I told you, we didn't have the evidence to make an arrest."

"Yeah, well there are always ways around that, aren't there? Maybe if you learned to play the angles a little, you'd catch more of these creeps than you let go."

She almost reminded him of his own dismal solve rate, but didn't bother. What was the point?

She laid the fresh sheets on the bed, tucked one of his pillows under her chin and began slipping it into a new case. "I'm not interested in bending the law to get what I want. That kind of behavior is for hacks and has-beens."

"So I'm a hack now, is that it?"

"That isn't what I meant."

"That's exactly what you meant. If you're gonna come here just to insult me, stay home next time. I got enough problems in my life. I don't need your negative nonsense."

Kate almost laughed. Her father was one of the most negative creatures she'd ever encountered. Always had been. And being around him was like stepping into a toxic wasteland without a hazmat suit.

The only reason she came here was because on some primal level she felt she owed it to her mother, who had inexplicably loved this man for most of her short life.

Mitch grunted. "Just get the hell out of here already, will you? I'll have Elsie do the sheets." Elsie was the care provider Kate spent a good portion of her salary on. "Or maybe I'll just stay in this chair. I can't sleep anyway."

He began to cough then, reaching for the box of Kleenex on the table next to him. Despite his abuse, Kate instinctively went to help him, but he waved her off.

"Go on, get out of here. Go play super cop and solve your god-damn case if you think you can. Oh, and while you're feeling optimistic, why don't you check in with your ex, see if he's interested in a reconciliation."

Kate stiffened. That was a low blow even for dear old dad.

"You're hopeless."

"Yeah, that's me, all right. Hopeless. One lung gone and the other on the way. But what about you? You think comin' here twice a week is your ticket to heaven? God don't give a shit, sweetheart. If he did, you wouldn't have a house full of dead bodies to contend with."

Kate was in no mood for this. Turning away, she snatched her bag off the dresser, slung it over her shoulder, and headed for the door.

"So that's it? I give you a little heat and you run?"

She stopped and spread her hands. "You just told me to leave, Mitch. What do you want from me? Blood?"

He waved her off again. "Fine. Go. Do what you want. Just do me a favor next time and get here earlier. I got shows to watch."

With this, he picked up the remote in his lap, turned on the TV, and began flipping through the channels.

And like so many times in the past, Kate Messenger ceased to exist.

3

SHE DIDN'T OFTEN VISIT CRIME scenes so late at night, but after circling the city to cleanse her mind, Kate found herself taking the 33 into the valley, as if something was drawing her there.

She had no idea what.

The Branford house sat at the end of a narrow road in the small suburb of Oak Grove, which was nestled in the mountains just east of Santa Flora.

Thad Branford, a local custom cabinet maker, had built the house himself on an isolated piece of land that was heavily populated by oaks. The remoteness of the location had afforded the killer—or killers—enough time to be thorough, and quite savage. Examinations of the bodies had indicated that Branford's wife Chelsea and his oldest daughter Bree had been brutally raped after their skulls were crushed with a claw hammer. Results were inconclusive on the other two daughters—twins, who where only eight-years-old.

Kate had seen brutality before, but nothing quite like this. And she knew that the images of those bodies—or what was left of them—would linger for many years to come.

Most of the detectives on her squad who were privy to the details agreed with her father's assessment of the case. That there was a psycho killer on the loose. But, for now at least, Kate resisted the notion, thinking that this was exactly what the perpetrator wanted them to believe.

She may have been wrong. And probably was. She had nothing more than her gut telling her this. The evidence they'd gathered had been disappointing, to say the least—no unaccounted for blood or prints or semen traces. No usable DNA at all. Yet her instincts were reliable at least half the time, and she had decided to give them the benefit of the doubt and look more closely at the personal aspects of the case.

The problem was, the Branfords didn't seem to have any enemies. Thad Branford's employees thought he was a saint, and his friends at the local Rotary club had nothing but praise for the man. And his wife and children were well-loved in the community.

This wasn't evidence that could easily be dismissed, and it certainly pointed to the possibility that the murders *were* a random act. But Kate wondered if one of the Branfords had been singled out and the rest had merely been collateral damage or a calculated cover-up.

Could Chelsea have had an affair, and these murders were the handiwork of a jilted lover? And what about Bree? She was barely sixteen, but could she have been seeing someone outside her usual circle of friends who wasn't what he had seemed to be?

These were long shots—especially in light of all the interviews they'd conducted, and the telephone and computer records they'd poured over—yet neither was beyond the realm of possibility. And until Kate could eliminate them, she had no intention of turning this case over to the FBI profilers her poor excuse for a father so revered.

Despite the late hour, she wanted to take another look at the crime scene, and an even closer look at the wife's and daughter's personal belongings in the hope that something useful would jump out at her.

Something they had missed.

The only thing they'd found during the initial search that had raised any eyebrows was the variety of sex toys in Chelsea Branford's nightstand drawer. But this merely indicated that either the Branfords had an adventurous love life or Mrs. Branford was one frustrated woman.

Kate knew that finding anything new was a long shot, but she had to give it a try.

•

She had almost reached the house when she saw it: a beat-up old white Rambler station wagon parked on the side of the road not ten yards from the Branford driveway.

She slowed her SUV as she approached, and peered inside, but the Rambler was empty.

Was it abandoned?

It certainly looked that way.

On the other hand, what if it belonged to a reporter, or a couple of curiosity seekers, hoping to get a glimpse of the so-called House of Pain?

In the first couple days of the investigation, the media coverage had been relentless, and Kate had appeared on TV to request that viewers come forward with any and all information. But with the department otherwise remaining tight-lipped, and with the shock value of a celebrity death and a fresh new political scandal now dominating the airwaves, the murders had abruptly receded into the background to make room for these more important matters.

Which was just fine with Kate. It gave her a chance to move without the pressure of the press.

But there was always a straggler or two, usually the hardcore crime reporters, who weren't seduced by petty politics or celebrity gossip. And she hoped to God this car was abandoned. She didn't need the added headache.

She pulled her SUV into the Branford driveway, killed the engine, and scanned the area. There was no one lurking about, peering into windows—and that was a good sign, but not necessarily a definitive one.

The house itself matched its environment, looking much like an elaborate mountain cabin, an A-frame with knotted pine siding and a rustic, early pioneer vibe. But there was an attention to detail in the trim and deck rails and window treatments that revealed its owner's skill with wood, and Kate had no doubt that he'd been a terrific cabinet maker.

She opened her door and got out, looking past the yellow crime scene tape toward the deck and large bay window that dominated the front of the house. The glass reflected the moon and it was hard to see inside, but there was no sign of movement, and she saw no flashlight beams illuminating the blood spattered walls.

So maybe she *was* alone out here.

As a precaution, however, she unsnapped the holster at her hip for easy access to her Glock.

Better safe than sorry, as her mother used to say....

With this thought, a jumble of images filled Kate's mind—crime scene photos of her mother's battered corpse. When she first made detective, she had hoped to reopen what was now a very cold case, but she'd never been able to get beyond those photographs, a woman she loved more than anything, beaten and strangled and left between two Dumpsters. Over the years, she kept promising herself that she'd take another look one day, but that day had yet to come.

Shaking the images from her mind, she ducked under the tape and started across the drive toward the front deck, but stopped short when she caught sight of the door.

The lockbox attached to the knob hung open—the door itself ajar.

Kate was the one who had formulated the combination for that lockbox, and only the members of her team knew it.

So how had it been breached?

Feeling her heart kick up, she glanced back at the Rambler, knowing now that her hope that it was abandoned was nothing more than that. Someone—undoubtedly a reporter—was inside poking around in her crime scene, looking for something to juice up the story. As if it needed juicing.

But then another thought entered her mind.

What if it wasn't a reporter at all? Or even a curiosity seeker? What if it was the killer himself, doing what few perpetrators actually did: returning to the scene of the crime?

Was there something inside he wanted?

Something he hadn't found five nights ago?

A trophy?

Some evidence they'd missed?

Kate unholstered her Glock and hoped she hadn't been spotted, although the sound of her engine had been a pretty good indication that someone was outside.

Whoever was in there could be watching her right now, waiting for her to make a move. And common sense dictated that she turn around, get back in her car and call for help.

Stupid cops were often dead cops.

And Kate wasn't stupid.

She was about to start back to her SUV when something in the bay window caught her eye. She was at a different angle now, and the glare of the moon was less pronounced, shining light *inside* instead of back at her.

She thought for a moment that she must be seeing things, that her mind was mistaking shadow and light—and maybe a piece of furniture—for something other than it was.

But no.

A boy stood in the Branford's living room.

A boy in a hooded sweatshirt.

Crouching low, Kate pointed her Glock toward the door, then moved closer to the window, and peered inside.

The boy was small, maybe eleven or twelve. He stood square in the middle of the room, on a carpet stained with dried blood, an evidence marker at his feet—the spot where Alicia, one of the twins, had been found. He was rocking back and forth, staring straight up at the ceiling as if he were studying a crack or some water damage.

And his eyes. Even in the pale light, there was something unearthly about them. Dark corneas covered by a fine milky film.

Was he... blind?

Kate quickly scanned the rest of the room and saw nothing but furniture and shadows. The boy couldn't be the driver of the Rambler, so who was with him and where were they?

Knowing she should go straight back to her car, she decided that maybe she was stupid after all, because something about this boy compelled her to move forward.

Something... unexplainable.

And then it happened.

She heard a voice inside her head—a child's voice—like a distant, nebulous radio transmission from some other planet:

... Etak, olleh ...

The sound stopped her cold. What the hell?

She glanced around, saw no one else in the vicinity.

... Etak, olleh ... Diarfa eb t'nod ...

Tightening her grip on the Glock, she turned, looked at the boy again, then closed her eyes and shook her head.

She knew she'd been working too hard, but this was insane. This voice... this... whatever it was... had to be a product of stress and sleep deprivation and she needed to pull herself together.

Keeping the Glock raised, she opened her eyes again and waited, afraid for a moment that whatever she thought she'd just heard might return. Then she stepped past the window, put her back against the wall and sidled up to the door, nudging it with her toe.

As it swung inward, she shifted her weight and pivoted, quickly taking in her surroundings as she eased into the living room.

The place was empty and quiet, except for the boy standing in a pool of moonlight, still rocking back and forth, those unearthly eyes staring at the ceiling, his quiet breaths barely audible in the stillness.

Hyper alert, Kate studied him, wondering if she was hallucinating. "Who are you? What are you doing here?"

The boy said nothing. Showed no indication that he even knew she existed.

Was he deaf, too?

"Are you alone in here, or is there someone here with—"

"He won't respond to you when he's like that," a voice said.

Startled, Kate whipped around, training her Glock on a dark doorway to her right. The shadowy figure of a man stood facing her, and her skin prickled with surprise and sudden fear.

"Police," she told him as a spike of adrenalin shot through her body. "Don't you move. Don't you fucking move."

4

"I'M NOT ARMED," THE MAN said. "I don't even own a gun."

A vague hint of the South tinged his voice, a barely-there Appalachia that reminded Kate of an attorney she'd met years ago in one of her criminology classes.

Heart pounding, she unclipped the mini-mag from her belt and shone it at him.

Early to mid forties. Graying. A rugged, lived-in face. Hands tucked into the pockets of a faded Burr jacket. He squinted slightly against the light, but she noted a haunted quality to his dark eyes, and sensed they'd seen many of the same horrors hers had.

"Hands," she said tersely, gesturing with the Glock. "Show me your hands. Slowly."

He didn't resist, taking them out to show her they were empty.

"Now lift the jacket and turn around."

He lifted his jacket and spun slowly around, revealing no signs of a weapon. A pencil and a spiral bound notepad protruded a good four inches from his back pocket and Kate now thought she knew what she was dealing with.

She glanced at the boy, who was still rocking quietly and staring at the ceiling. Grabbing the back of the man's jacket, she shoved him up against the nearest wall, held the flashlight with her mouth, and gave him a quick pat down.

When she was done, she said, "Who are you? Are you a reporter?"

The man laughed softly. "No."

"Then what's with the notepad?"

"I always carry it with me."

That wasn't an answer, but she let it go. "What's your name?"

No response.

"I didn't find a wallet. Don't you carry one of those too?"

"I left it in the car."

"Of course you did."

She knew she should slap some cuffs on this guy and call for assistance, but something compelled her not to. She felt off her game and slightly disoriented and couldn't explain it.

Instead she released him and stepped back, keeping the flashlight and Glock trained on him as he turned around. "Move to the center of the room. Get next to the boy."

The man did as he was told as the boy continued to rock and stare at nothing.

Was he autistic? In some kind of trance?

He was really starting to creep her out.

They both were.

She gestured. "What's wrong with him?"

"Nothing. He's doing what he always does."

"Which is what?"

The man hesitated. "Gathering."

Kate had no earthly idea what that was supposed to mean. "What the hell are you talking about? What kind of fruitcakes are you two?"

She heard her father in that remark and didn't much like it.

"We don't want to cause trouble. We didn't expect anyone to be here."

"So you see the place is empty and decide to break in? Did you know the Branfords? Are you a friend of theirs? Family?"

The man shook his head. "I've already said too much."

"You haven't said a goddamn thing. Just tell me what you're doing here."

He didn't respond.

She kept the flashlight beam in his face. "What's your relationship to this boy? Are you his father?"

"Guardian," he said.

She'd heard that one before, and the creep factor multiplied exponentially.

She needed more than this damn flashlight. She needed the overheads on, and maybe the added light would bring the kid—and *her*—back from planet What-the-Fuck.

"Don't move," she said, then went to the wall and tried the switch. Nothing. She stepped past an overturned lamp stand, then crossed to an end table, tried the lamp there and got the same results. Either the power company had prematurely pulled the plug or these two had tampered with the electrical panel.

But to what end?

"Are we under arrest?" the man asked.

"What do you think? You're contaminating a crime scene."

"We haven't touched anything."

"Except the lock box, right? How long have you been here?"

"Maybe ten minutes or so."

"And does your little friend ever snap out of it or is he suffering from some kind of brain damage?"

The man made a face. "Why are you so hostile?"

"Gee, I don't know. Maybe because you don't belong here?"

"Look," he said, "I appreciate your caution, but I'm unarmed and I've done everything you've asked."

"Except answer my questions."

"Could you at least quit pointing that gun at me. I've seen what they can do too many times."

"Meaning what? Are you a cop?"

He laughed again and shook his head. "No."

"Then who the hell are you?"

"Nobody you need to be concerned with. I can promise you that."

"Forgive me if I don't feel reassured, Obi-Wan. You saw the yellow tape out there, yet you chose to ignore it. You know exactly what happened here. And if you don't tell me who you are and what the hell you're..."

The boy suddenly moved his head, shifting his sightless gaze from the ceiling to stare straight into the flashlight beam.

Straight at her.

... *Etak, yako s'ti* ...

And there it was again, that strange, nebulous radio transmission inside her mind—an odd foreign language that was impossible to translate.

... *Diarfa eb t'nod ... Uoy rof gnitiaw neeb ev'i* ...

What the hell was happening to her?

Kate took a step backwards and then the boy's entire body started to quake, shimmying and shaking as he stood in place. The overhead lights flickered on, then went out again as his knees buckled and he fell to the floor, his back arching, his feet twisting, his body bucking wildly.

Shit.

A seizure. He was having a seizure.

The man dropped to a crouch beside him and began loosening his clothes.

"A towel!" he shouted. "I need a hand towel or a wash cloth—quick."

Kate was at a loss. "For what?"

"I don't want him to swallow his tongue. Check the bathroom—please!"

Kate didn't need any further prompting. Tucking her Glock in its holster, she rushed through the side doorway into the hall, using the mini-mag to light her path. She'd been in this house enough times to know exactly where the bathroom was—at the far end and to the right.

She got to it and barreled inside—a cavernous place with double sinks and a Toto toilet and wood everywhere, with the same attention to detail as the outside trim and window treatments. This was one of three bathrooms in the house and stood adjacent to the two younger daughters' bedrooms, and Kate could see them in here, getting ready for school every morning, fighting over who got to shower first—a ritual that had ended five nights ago in the most brutal fashion imaginable.

She dashed to the linen closet in the corner and threw it open, using the flashlight to illuminate the stacks of towels, searching until she found the shelf holding the wash cloths.

She snatched one up and as she turned to leave, it suddenly struck her—

Wasn't that whole swallowing your tongue thing a myth?

Emergency response was part of every officer's training, but that had been a long time ago and she'd be damned if she could remember. She was a major crimes detective, used to dealing with burglars and rapists and dead bodies, not victims of epileptic seizures. But she had a feeling she'd just been conned, and conned good.

Fuck.

Stupid cops were also often embarrassed cops, and she had just won the gold medal for morons.

Yanking her Glock free again, she lit out, nearly bouncing off the walls as she hurtled back down the hallway, ready to open fire if that creep or his kid tried to intercept her.

But they didn't.

To nobody's surprise, when she got back to the living room they were gone, nowhere to be found, and Kate heard a car engine firing up outside.

The Rambler.

She glanced toward the window, saw its headlights go on, then dashed through the front doorway and onto the deck, raising the Glock with both hands.

"Stop!" she shouted. "Stop right now!"

But they didn't stop. The Rambler lurched forward and made a quick U-turn as Kate ran into the drive and blew past the yellow crime scene tape.

"Stop, goddamn it!"

She was tempted to fire, but knew she couldn't, not with a kid sitting in the back seat.

How would she explain that?

Instead, she focused on the license plate, which was barely legible in the moonlight. It was an original from NORTH CAROLINA, black and yellow, the words DRIVE SAFELY stamped across the top. She committed the tag number to memory, trying one last shout for good measure—

"Stop!"

But she was wasting her breath. The Rambler came perilously close to burning rubber as it dug out and disappeared down the road.

Kate lowered her weapon, letting loose a string of angry curses. She was a veteran cop, for Christ's sake, the head of her squad, yet she'd felt out of sorts from the moment she got here and had handled herself like a ham-handed amateur.

And she could almost hear her father cackling with glee.

5

IT WAS THE BOY, SHE decided. The boy who had thrown her off. Those eyes and that odd, rocking trance and that nebulous radio transmission that had filled her head—which she knew was impossible—yet felt as if it had come directly from him.

Etak, yako s'ti.

There had been more, but that was all Kate could remember, and she wasn't sure she even had *that* much right.

Etak, yako s'ti.

And the sound of it—that *sound*—a language that seemed so familiar, but was impossible to place.

Jesus—was she losing her mind?

Easy, Kate. Take it easy.

You're fine. You're golden. You aren't losing anything.

Stress. That's what this was. From the case, and her father dying, and her guilt over hating him... And then there was her failed marriage, and the thoughts of her mother's battered corpse
—

—and that boy. That strange, yet compelling boy.

Even the best cops have an off day, and while she was better than most, she didn't come close to being the best. She knew that.

Though she tried. God knew she tried.

Come on, Kate. Man up, pull it together, grow some gonads. You blew the play, so quit your whining and make it right.

Sitting in her car now, she took a deep breath, reached for the mic on the dash and radioed the dispatcher, giving him a description of the vehicle and its occupants and the number of the North Carolina license plate.

A decrepit old Rambler should be easy enough to spot. And before long, she'd have the boy and his evasive creep of a guardian in custody, and then the real interrogation would begin.

It might not solve her case...

...but it was bound to be interesting.

6

IT PROBABLY WASN'T A GOOD idea to be playing games with the police.

As they drove out of Oak Grove and headed back toward the city, the man thought about their impromptu bit of theater, and part of him admired their quick thinking. But it wasn't wise to mess with law enforcement. They needed to be careful. To stick to the shadows. To fly low and stay off the radar to prevent any impediment to their progress.

He and the boy had spent the last ten months managing to *avoid* confrontations. And now, thanks to an overzealous detective, they would have to go underground for awhile. And stay there until they were little more than a forgotten entry in the Santa Flora law enforcement database.

Which meant ditching this wagon, of course, the car Anna had so loved.

But maybe it was time for a change. The man had done his best to keep the Rambler running, but the road had begun to take its toll. It killed him to give it up—one of the last links to the life he'd once known—but he'd do what had to be done. He and the boy couldn't afford to be caught. They were sharks, who could not slow down, could not stop until they had their prey in their jaws. Until they had devoured him, just as he had devoured their past.

The man cursed himself for not being more aware of his surroundings back at that house. He'd been in one of the back rooms and hadn't heard the detective's car pull into the drive. And by the time he returned to the living room to check on the boy, it was too late. She was already coming through the door.

He'd have to learn to stay more alert. Not only to avoid the police, but to be ready in case the unthinkable happened. In case the roles they had chosen for themselves were reversed, and the hunters became the hunted.

Because next time it might not be the police coming through the door.

Next time it might be someone far worse.

●

Shortly after they rolled onto the Interstate, the boy sat up in the back seat.

We should have turned by now. Where are you going?

"We can't stop," the man said. "We'll be drawing heat for what happened. We can't go back to the motel."

What about our bags? Our clothes?

The man hated when the boy got like this. He was usually so calm and so eerily self-assured. "We'll get new ones."

But what about my photo book? I need my photo book.

Ahh, yes. The man had forgotten about that. That photo book was the *boy's* only link to his former life. He had spent many nights curled up on motel beds, the small, pink album clutched to his chest, the name *Lucy* written across the cover with a blue permanent marker. Every so often he would press his nose against it and smile, as if he were breathing in the best parts of his past.

And maybe that was exactly what he was doing. Maybe the smell of the cheap plastic conjured up images in his mind. Took him back to a time when all was good in the world.

To deny him that small pleasure was cruel.

But what choice did they have?

The man didn't doubt that the detective had already called in a description of the Rambler. And even worse, she may have managed to get the license plate number. They needed to be gone, as quickly as possible.

It was probably too late to catch a train. But according to his map, there was a station in West Santa Flora that also doubled as a bus depot. They could ditch the car, hole up there and catch the red-eye bus to Los Angeles, where they could stay lost long enough to figure out their next—

Turn around!

The boy's shout was like a needle piercing the brain.

Turn the car around!

There was a ferociousness to the sound he had never heard before. A ferociousness laced with desperation.

Turn it around! Turn it around!

TURN IT AROUND!

Hot white heat stabbed at the man's skull and he grabbed his head with one hand as he jerked the wheel and pulled to the side of the road. Stomping on the parking brake, he spun in his seat and scowled at the boy, whose own face was twisted in agitation.

"What the hell is wrong with you?"

The boy shrank back and the man immediately regretted the harshness of his tone. He never wanted this child to be afraid of him. No child should ever be afraid.

"I'm sorry," he said, still feeling the remnants of the pain. "But that last one nearly made my head explode."

The boy was breathing rapidly, but seemed to have calmed a bit.

You don't understand. I can't leave without my photo book. I have to have it. Please.

"But what if they're already looking for us?"

I don't care. I need that book.

The man was certain they'd regret this, but he did understand. The boy had already had so much taken away from him. They both had.

"All right," he said. "We'll go back, but we need to make it fast. I want to get rid of this car and be gone as soon as possible."

Thank you, the boy said. *Thank you.*

"And one more thing. I will never hurt you, okay? You never have to worry about that."

I know.

"Do you? Because it's important to me that you do."

I do. I know.

"Good," the man said.

Then he faced front again, released the handbrake and drove toward the nearest exit.

7

THE NIGHT SHIFT AT THE East Division of the Santa Flora Police Department consisted of two dispatchers, eight uniformed patrol officers, and a single detective who spent most of the night napping at his desk in the Major Crimes squad room.

Santa Flora was a large and thriving Central California beach town that attracted thousands of tourists daily. Most of the crimes it saw involved minor theft or break-ins or domestic disputes. And while murders and other serious crimes were rare compared to the surrounding cities, there were enough to justify a ten-deputy detective squad, of which Kate had recently taken the lead.

She had inherited the job from Russell "Rusty" Patterson, an old school veteran known mostly for his knack for departmental PR and a long string of successful solves. These were largely due to the men and women who worked under him, and Rusty was always happy to give them credit. But if you ever took part in a Rusty Patterson investigation, you'd find your name in the small print while he grabbed the headlines. And the public ate it up.

After fifteen years heading Major Crimes for the East Division, Patterson had finally retired, and the competition to fill his shoes had been fierce. Kate had won the job largely on the basis of Rusty's recommendation, but despite her screw up tonight, she liked to believe she was also the most qualified candidate. She'd been with the department for more than a decade, and had long been one of Rusty's top investigators.

Her ascension to his throne, however, had not come without a price. The reaction to her promotion had been swift and brutal and she'd once again found herself orphaned, this time by several of the men under her command. They did their jobs and followed orders, but only grudgingly. And Kate couldn't remember the last time she'd been asked to grab a beer.

But, unlike Rusty, she didn't care about headlines. She just wanted to do her job and leave the glad-handing to the Public Relations Division where it belonged.

•

Kate knew she should have gone home to get some sleep, but just after midnight she found herself wandering into the squad room, still feeling a little out of sorts.

Billy Zimbert, the night man, was awake for a change, nursing a cup of coffee as he surfed the Internet.

He stiffened at the sight of her. "Hey, lieutenant, what're you doin' here so late?"

Billy had never seemed to have a problem with Kate's rise in the ranks, but he was the biggest slacker in the division and probably didn't feel too comfortable having his new boss drop by in the middle of his shift.

Kate had always thought of him as something of a creeper and was glad he worked nights. There was a ghoulish quality to the guy that made her want to keep her distance.

"Nothing for you to be concerned about, Billy. Just go back to doing whatever it was you were doing."

He grinned, showing yellow teeth. "Just catching up on my coffee quota. It's kinda slow tonight. You want a cup? I'll go get you one."

She shook her head. "I just want to log some evidence and hit the databases. I had a little encounter out at the Branford house I want to check into."

"What kind of encounter?"

She thought about this and decided to downplay the incident. She still wasn't sure what had happened out there. "Couple of rubberneckers. I'm sure it's no big deal."

She started for her office, then stopped and looked at him. "You wouldn't happen to know how to hack a cell phone would you?"

After calling in the bulletin on the Rambler, Kate remembered why she had originally gone to the Branford house and went back inside to look around. She came away with an item that should have been collected on day one of their investigation: a pay-as-you-go smart phone she'd found in Bree Branford's bedroom.

The thing had been hidden in a zippered battery compartment of a mechanical stuffed bear that sat on a shelf next to Bree's bed. Kate had lifted the bear to look at a photograph lying beneath it (a shot of Bree and her two little sisters), and felt something shift inside.

She had assumed it was a battery pack, but decided to check anyway and hit pay dirt. Nobody would hide a cell phone unless there was something on it worth hiding.

Unfortunately, the phone was locked. She'd tried a few standard passwords—Bree's birthdate and "123456" and "password1"—but none of them worked. So she knew she'd have to turn it over to their computer forensics guy unless Billy was some kind of techno-wiz.

"Me?" he said. "I still have trouble with microwaves and garage door openers."

Kate heaved a mental sigh. Why wasn't she surprised?

She sometimes wished life moved at the pace of movies and television shows, where information was instantaneous thanks to super computers and massive databases and nerds who could hack their way past impenetrable firewalls in a matter of seconds. But real life was slow and cumbersome and fraught with misfires and blind alleys. And murder investigations often took months or even years, and usually wound up in a box in the Open Unsolved storage room—just like her mother's case.

Kate didn't want that to happen with this one. Not because she had to prove herself as Rusty Patterson's successor, but simply because she wanted the Branfords to have their justice.

Every victim deserved that.

•

As she waited for word on her APB, Kate went to her office and entered the Rambler's plate number into the national database. She got a hit immediately and found it was owned by a Noah and Anna Weston of Danbury, North Carolina.

She pulled up the Westons' driver's licenses and there he was— the man from the Branford house. He looked younger and a good deal happier, but was the same guy she'd encountered tonight, no question about it.

He seemed so clean cut in the photograph. Like somebody's

older brother or father or husband, who led an unremarkable but contented life. An attractive family man who cherished his loved ones and went to church every Sunday and taught his children to be respectful of their elders.

Of course, Kate was extrapolating, but that's what cops did until they had all the facts in front of them. And if she had met this version of Weston in a bar somewhere, she probably wouldn't have said no to the offer of a drink. After she had checked his ring finger.

Weston's driver's license was valid for another year, but the wife, Anna Weston—a freckle faced redhead who was quite beautiful in an earthy, down home way—had let hers expire several months ago and hadn't yet renewed it.

So why was that?

And how did the boy fit in?

Kate was about to switch over to the NCIC database to see if either Weston or his wife had a record, but stopped short when her cell phone began to ring.

She pulled it from her back pocket and answered it. "Messenger."

"Hey, Kate, it's Rodney in dispatch. We got a hit on your APB."

Kate sat upright. "Where?"

"Circle Eight Motel on Pacifica Avenue. Officer Halperin called it in. He's holding the two suspects in their room. Says they were in a hurry, packing to leave."

"Good," Kate said, getting to her feet. "Tell him to stay put. I'm on my way."

8

PACIFICA AVENUE WAS SANTA FLORA'S motel row. Choose the right establishment and you might get an actual view of the Pacific ocean. Choose wrong and you'd be stuck near the 101 Freeway with the smell of exhaust overpowering what little sea breeze blew in your direction.

The Circle Eight was one of the wrong choices.

Kate pulled up next to four haphazardly parked black-and-whites, cut her engine and got out. Patrol officers tended to gather like flies at the slightest hint of excitement, and three unis stood shooting the breeze outside the open door to Room 127.

They stopped talking when she approached. Kate nodded to them and got a curt "Hey, lieutenant" as she stepped through the doorway and went inside.

The fourth uniform—Halperin—stood near the bathroom door, keeping a watchful eye on his detainees.

Noah Weston was seated on one of the two twin beds, while the boy sat in a chair next to a small round table, his sightless eyes staring at nothing as he quietly rocked.

Both were cuffed.

Kate resisted the urge to plant her forehead in her palm and gestured to the boy. "Really, Halperin? He's like eleven years old. And blind."

"Hey, I don't make assumptions. Stupid cops are—"

"—dead cops. I know the mantra. Now get those things off him, for Christ's sake. If he starts beating you down, I'll take full responsibility. I might even try to stop him."

Halperin made a face. "Whatever you say, lieutenant."

His voice was laced with undisguised contempt, and Kate knew that Halperin, like many officers, didn't appreciate being chastised by a female. People loved to pretend that the department had changed, but it really hadn't. She'd been battling misogynists since *she* was one of the flies.

As Halperin stepped past her, she looked at the open suitcase and backpack sitting atop the vacant twin bed. The suitcase was small and worn and obviously belonged to the boy. Its contents consisted of T-shirts and jeans and tighty whities, along with a couple of YA books in brail and a small, square pink folder that looked like a child's photo album.

She picked up the album, then shifted her attention to Weston, who sat quietly on the other bed, looking fatigued and unhappy.

Very unhappy.

She was again struck by his haunted eyes. "I'm no expert in theater, Mr. Weston, but I have to say that you and your young friend are very good actors."

"Didn't do us much good, did it?"

"Not really, no. I'm always curious about people who decide that running from the law is a better option than cooperation."

She looked at the photo album in her hands and saw the name *Lucy* scrawled across it in blue pen. A child's handwriting.

The boy's? That didn't seem likely.

"And what would cooperating have gotten us?" Weston asked. "We weren't hurting anyone, but you said yourself you were planning to arrest us."

"Maybe if you'd given me a straight answer that wouldn't have happened."

Weston pushed out a breath. "You people are good at coming in after the fact, making all kinds of accusations, but somehow you never manage to do anything significant toward solving an actual crime. You go for the convenient target and ignore the obvious if it doesn't fit your scenario."

"I take it this isn't your first encounter with law enforcement?"

"You don't know?"

"Should I?"

"You know my name, I'm thinking you must know everything about me by now."

Kate smiled. "As surprising as this might be, you're not the only problem I have to contend with. But now you've got me curious.

Very curious. If I type Noah Weston into the NCIC database, what will I find?"

He said nothing, but the silence spoke volumes. Kate glanced at the boy, figuring she knew exactly what she'd find. The thought of this creep taking advantage of *any* kid was bad enough, but a boy who was blind and possibly autistic?

Deplorable.

She again looked at the photo album in her hands, this time flipping it open to take a look inside. She found only a single photograph, and was surprised to see that it was a bland, staged family photo of a man, woman and child—the kind printed on slick paper that comes with every album or picture frame. Either the real photos had been removed, or none had ever been added.

So why did the boy have it?

Especially since he couldn't see.

She looked at his so-called guardian. "Well, Mr. Weston? I asked you a question. Have you been in trouble before?"

Weston hesitated, as if he was about to enter a verbal minefield and needed to proceed with caution. "Not exactly. No."

"Why don't you translate that into something meaningful?"

He shook his head. "You've already made your mind up about me and you're just waiting for me to say something to confirm it. So I think I'll pass."

Kate sighed. "All right, then. Why don't we put you in a cell for the night and see how you feel about it in the morning?" She turned to Halperin. "Take him into the station and process him. I'll wait here for CPS to arrive."

Halperin didn't grace her with a response. He simply gestured for Weston to stand up, then took him by the arm and escorted him toward the door.

Before they reached it, Weston said to Kate, "Be gentle with the boy. He's been through a lot."

Kate held up a hand, stopping them. "You want to elaborate on that?"

"People are sometimes afraid of him because he's different," Weston said. "But he's a good kid."

"What's his name?"

Weston hesitated again, obviously reluctant to give up even the tiniest piece of information. But he finally gave in. "Christopher."

"Christopher what?"

Weston said nothing, and she knew he was done cooperating. She gestured for Halperin to take him away.

As they headed out, she went to the door and asked one of the flies outside to step in and observe. She then turned to the boy, wondering if he was even aware of what was going on.

He was as eerily quiet as ever. Still rocking. Back and forth. Back and forth.

"So what do you say, Christopher? Do you feel like talking to me?"

The boy didn't react, and unless he was indeed autistic, deaf—or both—she suspected he had been trained to remain silent.

She crossed the room and crouched in front of him, facing him at eye level. She placed a hand on his and he flinched, but he didn't stop rocking.

Kate said, "Mr. Weston is gone now and there's nothing to be afraid of. I just want to know a little about you."

For a fleeting moment she worried she might again hear that odd, radio transmission in reply, but assured herself that whatever psychological glitch had overtaken her earlier was no longer a concern.

At least she hoped it wasn't.

"Did he hurt you?" she asked. "Is that why you're afraid to talk?"

The boy still didn't respond.

"What about that little trick you played on me back in the house, with the seizure and the lights? Was that your idea, or have you and Mr. Weston done that before?"

Nothing.

Kate thought about pushing a little, but decided against it. Maybe Child Protective Services could get through to him.

She patted his hand and stood, returning her attention to their belongings on the bed, this time unzipping the backpack for a look inside.

She found more T-shirts and underwear—adult sized—a pair of worn jeans, a dog-eared paperback called *The History of Luminous Motion*, and some Triple-A road maps. A *lot* of road maps, well worn and rubber banded together in stacks of three.

She flipped through them and saw a combination of cities and states—California, San Francisco, Oregon, Washington, Portland, Vancouver, Nevada and several from other parts of the country. The Midwest. East. Some south. And, finally, one of the entire USA and Canada.

Either Weston was a dreamer or he and the boy had been on one hell of a road trip. And they'd been doing it old school, without the aid of a GPS.

The question was why?

Were they running from something?

And why had they wound up in Oak Grove, standing in the middle of her crime scene?

These were questions to be answered in the morning, assuming Weston would cooperate. But by then she'd know what he was hiding and have considerably more leverage.

Stuffing the maps back into the backpack, she turned and looked at Christopher. Rocking. Rocking. Back and forth. Back and forth. And she wondered what was going on inside his head. He seemed to exist in his own private bubble.

Whether it was by choice or by intimidation was another question she hoped to answer.

But that would have to wait.

9

TEN MINUTES LATER, A CPS case worker arrived and took Christopher with her. The boy would be given a place to sleep for the night, then brought to the station house first thing in the morning, for a physical exam and a more extensive interview—assuming that was possible.

Kate bid him a good night, got no response, and watched them drive away. Then she put Weston's backpack and the boy's suitcase in the back of her SUV.

After one last look around the motel room, she dismissed the patrol officers, crossed to the Rambler, which was parked a few yards away, and did a quick search. She found a couple fast food sacks that hadn't yet been tossed, a ratty wool blanket folded in the rear of the wagon, and a few gas receipts in the glove box.

She also found Weston's notepad, lodged between the bucket seats. She pulled it free and flipped it open, using her mini-mag to illuminate the pages.

What she saw both surprised and puzzled her. It wasn't a reporter's notepad at all, but a small sketchbook full of meticulous drawings.

And Weston was an amazing artist. The sketches—rendered only in pencil—were as lifelike as anything she had ever seen. But his choice of subject matter seemed random to her:

—A motel key with the number 493 on it.

—A train ticket stub marked PROVIDENCE, RI.

—A man's wrist sporting a crude tattoo of a circle with a black dot in the center.

—A road sign that read   WELCOME TO GEORGIA, STATE OF ADVENTURE.

—A hand clutching a Gideon Bible.

—A spouted canister marked FLAMMABLE.

And eyes. Lots of eyes. Some isolated, some showing part of a man's face that was ill-defined yet somehow unnerving.

There were dozens of these drawings, along with handwritten notes—numbers, names of cities, people, biblical citations, symbols...

The most recent page featured sketches of two Santa Flora landmarks—the clock tower from the Sandy Point Mall, which had been around since the sixties, and Amelia's Oak, a massive tree near the 33 that was planted in the early 1900s in honor of the slain daughter of a local politician.

Taken as a whole, Kate might have looked at this sketchbook as the work of a mad man, but it didn't strike her that way. The sketches were random, yes, but they didn't have the feel of a scattershot mind. They were precise and detailed, a chronicle of Weston's travels, the things he'd seen over a period of many months.

Weston was simply an artist who was fascinated by the mundane. Everyday objects and places and people were rendered with an uncanny perfection.

Who the hell *was* this guy?

.

After bagging the receipts and sketch pad, Kate stored them in her SUV, then drove home to her one-bedroom walk-up in East Santa Flora.

She wasn't prone to taking tub baths at two in the morning, but she drew a hot one and soaked in it for half an hour before going to bed. She considered getting on the computer to check into Weston's background, but decided it could wait until she'd gotten some rest.

She spent the next several minutes on her back in bed, staring at the ceiling, thinking about the boy, and the man, and the Branfords lying in pools of their own blood, their skulls shattered by a claw hammer...

Then she finally drifted off to sleep.

10

SHE WAS AWAKENED BY HER father just after six a.m.

He always called her on her landline, which was located right next to her bed.

She fumbled for it, put the receiver to her ear and was about to mumble a greeting when he cut her off.

"I was up all night thinking about tongues," he said, his wheezy, phlegm-choked voice sounding even more labored than usual. "I can't stop thinking about those goddamn tongues."

Kate, still groggy, groaned into the mouthpiece. "What the hell are you talking about, Mitch? Do you know what time it is?"

"Those victims up in Tacoma, remember? The ones in the house fire? They were all missing their—"

"Yeah, I remember. But what's it got to do with me?"

"It's a signature. A lot of these guys like to sign their work."

"I'm aware of that. Anyone who reads or watches movies or TV shows or has managed to make it past fifth grade is aware of it. What's your point?"

"I'm just wondering about your guy. What's his signature? You didn't find any missing tongues, did you?"

Kate sighed. "Seriously? This is what you woke me up for?"

"It's six o'clock, your highness. You shoulda been up an hour ago."

"This conversation is over."

"Cut your old man a break, for chrissakes. Because if any of your victims had their tongues cut out—"

"Goodbye, Mitch."

"—you could be dealing with a traveling psychopath—"

"I'm hanging up now."

"—and maybe a closer look at Tacoma will—"

She cradled the phone.

She knew Mitch was only trying to keep his mind active rather than allow himself to fall into the stupor of the damned, but the truth of the matter was that there were no missing tongues in the Branford house massacre and certainly no fires. She highly doubted the two crimes were connected.

In fact, she was sure they weren't.

And while she didn't mind sharing general case details, she wasn't about to get into the nitty gritty and have to listen to her father tell her how to run her investigation. Because the truth was, he had never been very good at police work, prone to looking for easy solutions based on wild speculation.

One day, out of curiosity, Kate had spent some time in the department's computer archives, looking at Mitch's old files and case notes, and had found that his approach to a crime was singularly narrow-minded and often misguided. Reading those files had been an education in how *not* to investigate a crime, and she wondered how he'd managed to survive in the job long enough to retire.

Most of the substandard work had come after her mother's death, and she had to wonder if the murder had blinded him to the possibility that there might actually be a few innocent people out there.

Mitch rarely talked about her mother, but when he did, Kate sensed a burning frustration inside him that had never been relieved. And maybe that frustration had fueled his abysmal career.

Whatever the case, Mitch's apparent obsession with the idea that the Branford killings were the work of a serial perp only solidified Kate's thinking that her current instincts were correct. That this was a one-off crime made to *look* like something far more sinister.

She supposed she could tell her father this in an attempt to shut him up, but suspected it would have the opposite effect, and he would only ridicule her, as he had so often in the past.

Besides, it felt much better just to hang up on him.

Once the receiver was on the cradle, she lay back, closed her eyes, and let these thoughts run through her mind as she tried to go back to sleep. She managed to doze fitfully for another hour, but at a quarter after seven she finally climbed out of bed and made herself a nice big cup of caffeine, hoping she'd be able to function on just three hours sack time.

She had once been involved in an investigation and pursuit—led by the inimitable Rusty Patterson—that had kept her up for nearly two days straight. So the thirty or so hours of sleep she'd managed to grab since the slaughter at the Branford house were something of a luxury.

So why didn't she feel rested?

11

BY EIGHT-THIRTY, KATE WAS IN the department parking lot when she heard a familiar voice call out to her.

"Katie?"

Her gut tightened and she stopped in her tracks and turned.

Coming toward her from across the lot was the man she had shared a house and a bedroom with for nearly six years.

Her ex-husband. Dan Brennan.

Four of those years had been good ones. The last two not so much.

"Glad I caught you," he said. "I've been assigned to the case you called in last night."

Santa Flora County statutes required that all suspected victims of child abuse undergo a physical examination before any formal police interviews could take place. A pediatric psychiatrist, Dan had been consulting with Child Protective Services for as long as Kate had known him. She had expected their paths to cross at some point, but not so soon after the divorce.

All she could think was, why now?

"You couldn't have declined?"

"Come on, Katie, you know the department is stretched to the limit. Let's just be professional about this and do what needs to be done."

He was the only one who called her Katie but it no longer warmed her. "Where's your assistant?"

Dan made a face. "So much for professional."

"I'm just thinking you may need her to whisper reassuringly in your ear or laugh at one of your stupid jokes or maybe soothe your tired and aching bones after a hard day's work. Who knows, maybe you'll even get a happy ending. That's certainly more than I got."

She was surprised by the venom in her voice, but she was still raw and didn't much feel like hiding it.

"Oh, for godsakes, Katie. Is this what it's come to?"

"What do you want from me, Dan? Do you expect me to pretend we never happened?"

"Maybe this *was* a mistake."

"One of many."

"Well there isn't much we can do about it at this point. I just spoke to the foster care volunteers. The child has been fed and prepped and should be here any minute now. So why don't we concentrate on the matter at hand and you can take comfort in knowing that *I* know exactly what you think of me."

"Oh, we've only scraped the surface, sweetie."

He studied her a moment. "Get some help, okay?"

"From some therapist who's just as screwed up as I am? No thanks."

"Get some sleep, then. You're starting to make your father seem like the happy-go-lucky charmer in the family."

"Fuck you," she said.

He grimaced, nodded, then pushed past her and headed for the entrance. "I'll grab you as soon as I'm finished with the exam."

"Don't hurry on my account."

12

WHEN KATE REACHED THE SQUAD room, one of the uniforms told her that Noah Weston had been brought up from his holding cell and put in an interrogation room.

She took a detour on her way to her office and stepped into the observation booth to look at him through the one-way glass.

She had expected to find him still agitated and angry, but the man she saw sitting at the interview table seemed to have found his bliss and looked as calm as a theta level Zen master.

Weston was facing her directly, and even the haunted eyes seemed clear and calm—almost disconcertingly so—and she wondered for a moment if she had misjudged the guy.

Were those the eyes of a child molester?

Hard to say. But if she *had* misjudged him, why had he been so reluctant to answer her questions last night? And why did his mistrust of law enforcement seem to run so deep?

There were a lot of *whys* with this one. The biggest being his presence at her crime scene.

What had he and Christopher been up to?

Gathering, he'd told her.

Whatever that meant.

His refusal to talk had infuriated her, but maybe once she knew more about him and was able to confront him with his past, he'd be more forthcoming.

Or maybe he'd lawyer up and call it a day.

It wouldn't be a first.

As she exited the observation booth, she turned to find Matt Nava headed her way down the corridor. "Hey, lieutenant, I've been looking for you."

Matt worked computer forensics. He was a smart kid, and they got along well, and Kate often thought he'd make a great little brother, if she ever needed one. The kind who's eager to please but rarely annoying.

"What's up?" she asked.

"I cracked your passcode in about a minute and a half."

He produced an evidence bag containing the cell phone she'd found in the stuffed bear at the Branford house, in the oldest daughter's bedroom. She had dropped it on his desk tagged URGENT, and with Weston crowding her mind, she'd forgotten all about it.

"That easy, huh? What was it?"

"Jesus."

It took her a moment to realize he was answering her question. "J-E-S-U-S?"

He nodded. "Number twenty-one on the greatest hits list."

Matt kept a tally of the most common passwords he encountered, all about as effective as a BandAid on a bullet wound.

"That's weird," she said. "I didn't get the impression the Branfords were religious. They didn't belong to any of the local churches. Maybe the daughter was a closet Christian."

"Or maybe not." He handed her the evidence bag. "I'm pretty sure she didn't use that password for the usual reasons. I think it's meant to be pronounced *Hey-soos*.'"

"What makes you say that?"

"Because that's the only name and number in her contacts folder and unless she's got a direct line to heaven, I'm figuring he's Hispanic."

The hairs on the back of Kate's neck started to prickle. "Is there a last name?"

Matt shook his head. "The call log shows a few dozen calls between them over the last couple months and nothing else. She never even ordered a pizza with the thing. So whoever this guy is, he was important to her."

No doubt, Kate thought.

So had she been right about Bree? Was this the secret boyfriend she had speculated about? Could this guy be the key to her case?

"What about text messages?"

"None. And no voice mail. Just the calls. Other than that, the phone's pristine."

Kate looked at it behind the plastic, a tremor of excitement rumbling through her. She needed to find out who this guy was.

"Thanks, Matt. I appreciate the help. And thanks for putting it at the top of your to-do list."

He shrugged and started away. "All in a morning's work, lieutenant. I usually go for the easy ones first."

If only Kate had that luxury.

13

AFTER MATT WAS GONE, KATE went straight to her office, dropped the evidence bag on her desktop, then pulled a pair of plastic gloves from her drawer and snapped them on.

She took the phone from the bag, hit the power button, waited for the thing to boot up, then keyed in the passcode.

J E S U S

A moment later she was scrolling through the call log to find that this guy Jesus was indeed the only name and number, no surname, no photo. There were forty-seven calls over the last two and a half months, sometimes several a day.

Kate knew that most kids today prefer text messages over phone calls, so the absence of any texts led her to believe that the two were being extra cautious about their communications. And forty-seven calls was some very serious airtime with a guy Bree had dedicated an entire phone to.

So who the hell was he?

A lover? A classmate?

A drug dealer?

Interviews with Bree's small circle of friends had yielded nothing of interest in the romance department. They all claimed she was unencumbered and happy to be, and mostly kept to herself when she wasn't hanging with them at school. Even her social networking on the Internet was limited to that same small circle, with no indication that she'd ever expanded it beyond those limited borders.

When it came to drugs and booze, Bree had been characterized by her closest friends as a "good" girl who would never get involved with such things. But it was Kate's experience that, out of respect for the dead, friends often painted the victim of violent crime in a much more virtuous light than he or she might deserve. And hiding a burner in a stuffed bear did not reflect virtue. Not to Kate's mind.

It was clear that Bree and Jesus had *something* going on, and she aimed to find out what it was. She just hoped his phone number didn't originate from another burner. That could make it difficult to trace.

Scooping up her landline, she punched through to ServCom, and after three rings, the line picked up.

"Services and Communications. Deputy Kelp. How can I help you?"

"Hey, Drew, Kate Messenger. I've got a number I need you to check into and—"

"The Branford case, right?"

Kate paused. "Yeah. How did you know?"

"Matt Nava over in ComFor made the request. I just got off the line with the provider. A local carrier, BC Wireless."

Good old Matt. Motivated but never obnoxious about it. "Did they cooperate?"

"Didn't even blink. I was about to give you a jingle when you called."

"Please tell me you've got good news."

"The phone isn't a throwaway, if that's what you're worried about, and the owner has a criminal record. You want the details now or should I send a link to his file?"

Kate could hardly believe how this morning was shaping up. The appearance of her ex-husband had been a downer, but here she was barely awake and both Nava and Kelp had already made more progress than her entire team had made in six days. A positive sign if there ever was one.

"Send me the link," she said. "And thanks."

After she hung up, she sank into her chair and flicked on her computer monitor.

Noah and Anna Weston's driver's licenses were still on the screen.

She stared at their images for a long moment, still trying to figure out how Weston fit into this puzzle—assuming he did at all—then finally minimized the window, called up her email and waited.

A few seconds later, Kelp's message came through.

She opened it and clicked the link and was taken to a department database file, a case history for one JESUS "CHUCHO" SORIANO, local resident, twenty-four years old.

Twenty-four?

This was getting more and more interesting.

Bree Branford had barely turned sixteen when she was raped and murdered. So why was a so-called "good girl" exchanging phone calls with a twenty-four year-old career criminal?

Because that's what Soriano was.

Kate scrolled through his history and found quite an extensive record of arrests, some solo, some gang related. Robbery, assault, terroristic threatening, pandering, all starting with a burglary in his late teens.

Yet despite all these arrests, only one had resulted in a conviction—the original burglary. All the other charges had been dropped for lack of evidence.

Which made no sense whatsoever.

Either "Chucho" Soriano was woefully misunderstood, had a damn good lawyer, or he was protected—somebody's CI.

Confidential informants went about their business with a certain amount of impunity as long as they provided valuable information to their handler. So if Soriano was a snitch, who was he working for?

The department's gang squad? The local police? The FBI?

Whatever the case, pursuing this lead was bound to ping somebody's radar. And not in a good way. But Kate had no choice. She needed to bring this guy in for questioning.

Reaching for her landline, she was about to tell the two juniors on her team to do just that, when there was a sharp knock at the door.

Before she could respond, it flew open and Detective Sergeant Bob MacLean strode into the room, looking like the overbearing bull he was. "You mind telling me what the fuck is going on in Interview A?"

So much for positive signs.

MacLean had been Kate's closest competition in the race to replace Rusty Patterson, and in the heat of battle he'd said a lot of nasty things behind her back. *Clueless cunt* was the gem that had resonated, and it wasn't long before his supporters had pegged her with the nickname "CC."

She and MacLean had been competing ever since their academy days, with MacLean claiming most of the trophies. But, clueless or not, Kate had snagged the big one and he just couldn't get over it.

"His name is Noah Weston," she said. "I caught him at the crime scene last night."

"The Branford house?"

"That *is* the case we're working, Bob."

MacLean frowned. "So why am I only finding out about it now?"

"Seriously? You want me to start calling you at one in the morning?"

"Be nice if you consulted me at all."

Kate had assigned MacLean and his partner to assist in the Branford investigation as a kind of olive branch. But now Bob took every opportunity to assert himself, and the sight of him just made her weary.

She sighed. "Give it a rest, all right? I'll brief you along with everyone else at our eleven o'clock."

The five detectives working the case—two junior and three senior—met every morning to discuss progress and strategy. So far, MacLean's contribution hadn't been particularly impressive and had, in fact, cost them a considerable amount of time.

Kate had never quite understood why Rusty had kept him on the squad, considering his attitude and methodology were about as misguided and simpleminded as her father's. But Rusty's reign was over now and, despite the olive branch, she knew it was time for a change.

MacLean didn't move. "So what happens in the meantime? You plan on talking to this guy?"

"He isn't here for a job interview."

"And you didn't think to invite me to sit in?"

"No, I didn't. This is a peripheral matter and you're about as delicate as a sledge hammer. I don't need you giving him another reason not to cooperate."

"So you just shut me out? Is that it?"

"Like I said, I'll get you up to speed at the eleven o'clock."

MacLean looked as if he'd swallowed something sour. "You really are a piece of work, you know that?"

"Careful, Bob, I'm starting to think you don't like me."

"Why the hell won't you just tell me what's going on?"

She could, but she wasn't going to. Maybe if he treated her with respect every once in awhile she'd give it right back, but she was tired of his bullshit. And truth be told, she enjoyed watching him dangle.

"You'll hear everything I have to say at the briefing. Now go grab yourself some coffee and a donut and relax. You look like you could use some down time."

MacLean glared at her for a good ten seconds and she knew he was raging inside. Then he gave up—*thank God*—and stomped out of her office, leaving the door open behind him.

Kate felt a smile coming on and knew she had to improve her people skills and learn not to be so petty.

Maybe he was right.

Maybe she *was* a piece of work.

And maybe the second half of that nickname was well deserved.

14

THIS WASN'T THE FIRST TIME Noah Weston had been left waiting in an interrogation room.

He knew from his brief experience in the past that he might be sitting here for hours before they finally got around to questioning him. It was a technique the police often used, leaving a suspect alone in hopes that his anxiety would build to a boil and he'd confess his way into a prison sentence.

That was what they'd tried to do back in Danbury.

Get Weston to confess.

They had known with an almost scientific certainty that he wasn't the man they were looking for, but narrow minded people tended to ignore the obvious and find motive and opportunity where none existed. And these same people were often attracted to the structure and security and sense of empowerment that careers in law enforcement had to offer.

Human nature taking its course.

So he knew what these people thought about him and the boy. But then he'd probably think the same thing if he were in their shoes.

Yet any anxiety he'd felt over the mistakes he'd made last night had long since abandoned him. He found that if he spent most of his time focusing on his task, on the work that lay ahead, everything else simply melted away and a sense of calm washed over him.

It was, he thought, a lot like prayer. Something he had once been intimately familiar with before God—or whoever—had decided He'd heard quite enough, thank you, and had delivered the message in as heinous a manner possible.

Weston hadn't prayed since, or spent a single moment in

church, and found no reason to. But focusing on their task—his and the boy's—was far better than any prayer he'd ever uttered. Focusing on their task did not allow him to fall victim to his own insecurities, and to the folly that some benevolent king was watching over him.

Unburdening himself of his superstitions had allowed Weston to do whatever he felt necessary in order to find and destroy the monster who had brought God's message to his home.

That day would come. He knew it in his gut.

And when it did, he would make his arrows drunk with blood.

15

BY THE TIME KATE WALKED into the interrogation room she was armed and ready.

After ordering the two junior detectives on her team to find and pick up Bree Branford's gangbanger phone buddy, she had returned her concentration to Noah Weston. She'd spent the good part of an hour checking into his background and looking through the items she'd taken from his motel room and car.

When she entered his name into the National Crime Information Center database and read the results, her internal alarm bell went off. What she discovered didn't explain why Weston and Christopher had been at her crime scene, but she now knew that they were much more than a couple of rubberneckers.

There was something seriously off about these two, and she aimed to find out what it was and how it related to the Branfords.

After closing the door behind her, she placed a file folder containing Weston's sketch pad and maps and receipts and database records on the table top, then pulled a chair out and sat across from him.

She was about to speak when he held up a hand, cutting her off. "Before you launch into whatever pitch you have planned, just tell me one thing."

She nodded. "I'm listening."

"What made you decide to become a police detective?"

She looked at him. "I don't see how that's relevant, Mr. Weston. Why don't we just—"

"It's relevant to me," he said.

She paused. "Why?"

"Just humor me. It's a harmless enough question."

She considered this then nodded again. If it would get him

talking, she was happy to oblige. "All right. I don't really think about it much, but I guess you could call it the family business. My mother was a dispatcher and my father was a cop. Major Crimes, just like me. In fact, he sat in this very same room a number of times."

"But it's more than that, isn't it?"

"What do you mean?"

"You lost someone to violence. I can see it in your eyes."

The remark threw Kate off guard, and she stared at him, wondering if he was psychic or if the burden she carried was that obvious. Her mother's murder had weighed heavily on her for a long time, but did she wear it like a banner? Did he see that same haunted look she'd seen in him?

She shifted uncomfortably. "That's really none of your business."

"Maybe so, but it's true. And believe it or not, that works in your favor."

"My favor, huh? So glad I could please you." She patted the file folder. "Now why don't we talk about the violence in *your* life? Tell me about Anna and your two little girls."

She had hoped the mention of his family would rock him, but he remained as calm as ever.

Had someone slipped him a couple Ativans in the holding unit?

"I see you've done your homework," he said.

"I have. And now I understand your animosity toward people like me."

"Can you blame me?"

She shrugged. "I don't imagine it's easy being accused of something so horrible, but it isn't uncommon for us to look at the husband and father first."

"I know how it works," Weston said. "The problem I have is when you *only* look at the husband and father. You make assumptions, then try to find evidence to back them up. That's the opposite of how it should work."

"Sometimes we have to go with our gut. And sometimes we get it wrong."

"At whose expense? The man who tried to take me down still thinks I'm guilty. Even though the forensics say I'm not."

"I know," Kate said. "I just got off the phone with him."

She had put a call into Charles Dillman, the Stokes County prosecutor who had handled the case, and had discovered that Weston was still their prime suspect.

"He claims the forensics were either botched or inconclusive. He also told me you initially lied about where you were that night."

"I had my reasons," Weston said.

"And if that reason hadn't come forward of her own accord, you'd probably be sitting in a North Carolina jail right now, instead of having this little chat here in sunny California."

"Is that what this is? A chat?"

"That's all it has to be if you tell me what you and your young friend were up to last night."

He said nothing.

"Look, Mr. Weston, I could sit here and pretend that I can't imagine what you've been through—but the thing is, I can. You were right, I've lost someone to violence and I know how devastating it can be. But what I saw in that house you and Christopher broke into was something else altogether. So I won't insult you by suggesting I have the slightest idea how it feels to find the people you love slaughtered like diseased cattle."

She was purposely trying to provoke a reaction again, but got none, and wondered what it meant.

If anything.

She pressed on. "But unless you start cooperating and tell me why you and Christopher came to Santa Flora, I'll have to wonder if maybe the Stokes County prosecuting attorney isn't that far off base about you."

A flicker of life behind the eyes now. "You think I'd butcher my own family?"

"Did you?"

Weston studied her. "I was hoping I was wrong about you, but I guess I wasn't." He leaned forward. "Are you going to charge me with something? Because if you aren't, I'd like to go."

She patted the folder again. "You're quite the artist. I took a look at your sketch pad and you have a rare talent. This kind of photo-realistic ability must have taken years to perfect. Even the doodles and notes have an artistic quality to them that most people would envy."

"They wouldn't if they knew why I do it."

"And why is that?"

Again, he was silent.

"It's a simple question, Mr. Weston. Why do you do it?"

He just stared at her and she could see he wouldn't budge, so she tried a different approach.

"All right. Let's talk about the boy instead. Tell me about Christopher."

"I told you. I'm his guardian."

"I assume he has a last name?" She smiled. "You know. The one you didn't want to give me last night?"

"Why does that matter?"

"Why do you think? I'm trying to determine who he is and why he's with you. What is he, a stray you picked up off the road?"

"He's with me because he wants to be."

"And why do I doubt that?"

"Because it's the nature of your profession."

"I assume you care about him?"

"Of course I do."

"Then why haven't you asked me where he is?"

"I don't need to."

"Oh? You've been separated for hours now. You're not curious to know where he spent the night? Or if he's scared?" She paused. "Or maybe you're worried he might finally decide to speak up."

"That's not likely to happen."

"You have him that well trained, do you?"

Weston shook his head. "You have no idea what you're talking about. I'm not worried about him because there's no reason to be. I already *know* where he is."

"And where is that?"

"Downstairs in the medical unit, undergoing a physical examination."

The answer surprised Kate. If he was guessing, it was a good one. "Who told you that?"

Weston didn't respond.

"You two have been through this before, haven't you."

He shook his head again. "You're wasting your time, lieutenant. You've seen my records, you know my history. I'm no more a pedophile than I am a murderer."

"You've never been charged—that's all I know. Maybe you're just very good at hiding it."

"Well, in a few minutes, Christopher's exam will be done and you'll get word that beyond his obvious physical limitations, he's as healthy as any kid his age, with no evidence of sexual abuse at all."

He spoke with a certainty that was almost unsettling.

"You seem pretty sure about that."

"I haven't lied to you yet."

"Like you did to the Stokes County prosecutor?" She smiled. "Truth is, you haven't said much of anything. All you do is play cryptic games. Why can't you just tell me what the two of you were doing last night? What was all that nonsense about gathering?"

"You wouldn't understand."

"Did you know the Branfords?"

"No."

"Do you know they were all murdered, much like your wife and kids?"

"Yes."

"Did you have something to do with that?"

He stared at her. "You can't be serious."

"Oh, I'm serious, Mr. Weston. How can you sit there and think I'm not? You were nearly put on trial for a crime eerily similar to what went down in that house, so I'd have to be a world class moron not to be pretty goddamn serious."

Weston looked unfazed. "I assume you found the receipts in my dash?"

"What?"

"When you searched my car last night. You found my sketchbook, you must've searched the dash, too." He nodded to the file folder. "You've probably got them in there somewhere."

"And if I do?"

"How long has it been since the Branfords were murdered?"

"I think you already know that."

He nodded. "Six days. And six days ago Christopher and I were staying at a motel in Reno. The credit card receipt should be in there. We also filled our gas tank and ate dinner at a drive-in called the Burger Barn. Those receipts will have the date and time stamped on them, but I'm guessing you're thorough enough to have already checked them."

He was right, and she had wondered briefly if they were elaborate forgeries. But that idea sounded more like bad fiction than anything based in reality.

"It looks as if the only thing you're serious about, lieutenant, is a desire to satisfy your curiosity. And I really have no interest in helping you with that. So do I need to get a lawyer in here or can Christopher and I be on our way?"

"And where would you go if I cut you loose?"

"That's really none of your business."

"I found the maps in your backpack. And there're those sketches of road signs and train tickets and landmarks. You two seem to be on quite a trek."

"Again. None of your business."

Kate slapped a palm on the table. "Goddamn it, Weston, how can you sit there acting as if this is just some leisurely lunch? What the hell is wrong with you?"

He didn't flinch. "I told you what's wrong. I don't like the police. I don't trust you and I don't like interacting with you. And not because of anything *I've* done, but because you tend to play God and make decisions about people's futures based on nothing more than supposition and paranoid fantasy."

Kate drew in a long breath and released it slowly. She needed to calm down. She was letting him get to her and that was never a good thing.

But when it came down to it, he wasn't wrong about her motives, and she knew she should be concentrating on Jesus "Chucho" Soriano instead of him. But there was something about this guy—and even more so the boy—that scratched at her insides. And she'd just as soon kick his ass than let him walk out of here.

She picked up the file folder and got to her feet. "You might as well get comfortable, because we aren't done yet. Not even close. So if you want that lawyer, just give me the word and I'll make it happen."

"Really? You plan to take it that far?"

"You seem to forget I've got you dead to rights on trespassing, obstruction, and resisting arrest. I can also hold you for forty-eight hours *without* charges. That's the way it works here in the Golden State. But you probably know that, too."

Weston sighed heavily, revealing a small crack in his demeanor. "What is it you want from me, lieutenant? You want me to tell you that Christopher and I are a couple of ghouls who get pleasure out of visiting grisly crime scenes? Then fine. That's why we were there."

Kate shook her head. "I don't believe that for a minute."

"Then go ahead and waste everyone's time and do whatever it is you have to do. Because that's all you're getting out of me."

He looked away from her, eyeing himself in the one-way glass, and if human beings had an off switch, he had just tripped it. He'd said all he was willing to say.

But Kate could be as stubborn as he was.

Without another word, she left the room and locked him inside.

16

SHE HADN'T BEEN JOKING WHEN she told MacLean to grab some coffee and a donut and wait for the morning briefing. The East Division was currently being renovated, with the conference room under repair for water damage, so she and her team had been forced to turn the employee break room into an impromptu command center for the duration of the Branford investigation.

At eleven o'clock each workday, they put a sign on the door, rolled out a portable white board from the supply closet, and closed everyone else out. For the next hour, the hardcore caffeine addicts were stuck with the backwater swill from the vending machine down the hall, and they were never shy about expressing their displeasure.

Kate sympathized, but what choice did she have?

She was five minutes late for this morning's meeting, and with her two juniors out tracking down Soriano, only MacLean and his partner Jake Linkenfeld were waiting for her.

Linkenfeld was a nice enough guy, who showed Kate the respect she felt she deserved, but if he hung around MacLean long enough, he was bound to be infected by the anti-CC virus. Unlike MacLean, he was a good, empathetic cop who had demonstrated some major investigative skills.

The two were sitting at their usual table, sharing a joke when she entered the room. She sat down across from them mid-laugh and planted Bree Branford's stuffed bear on the table top.

"What's this?" MacLean said with a nasty little grin. "You're new sex toy?"

Linkenfeld didn't dare laugh and Kate ignored the remark, looking straight at MacLean.

It was time to break the bad news.

"You were the one who searched Bree Branford's bedroom that first night, right?"

This was an uh-oh moment and MacLean knew it. His grin faded. "What about it?"

She nodded to the bear. "I assume you recognize this little guy?"

"Now that you mention it, yeah. It was on the shelf by her bed." He seemed proud of the fact that he remembered this.

Kate grabbed hold of the bear and flipped it over, showing him the unzipped battery compartment, then tossed the evidence bag containing Bree's cell phone onto the table.

"Looks like you missed something, Bob."

He stared at the phone. "You telling me that was inside?"

"That's where I found it."

"So... what? I'm supposed to be psychic? Anybody could have missed something like that. It could've been the battery, for chrissakes."

"Except it wasn't. And as it turns out, it's a pretty goddamn crucial piece of evidence."

"Why?" Linkenfeld asked. "What's on it?"

She told them about Bree's call log and Chucho Soriano's criminal record and added, "That's why Clark and Donohue aren't here right now. I sent them out to chase this guy down."

"Holy shit," Linkenfeld said. "So all this time we're thinking random psychopath and this creep's just sitting there waiting to be found."

"*You* two were thinking random psychopath. I told you from the start it didn't feel right." Kate turned to MacLean. "And if somebody had done his job, we would've known about this guy on day one. And we'd better hope to hell he hasn't skipped."

MacLean blanched. "You're blaming *me*?"

"No, Bob, I blame myself for putting you on this case in the first place. You're too arrogant for your own good and I should've known you'd find a way to screw us up."

"You fucking *bitch*."

Without warning, MacLean launched himself across the table toward Kate, and if it hadn't been for Linkenfeld, he would have reached her, too.

Jake grabbed hold of him and pulled him back as Kate pushed away from the table and sprang to her feet. "All right, that's it. You just made this very easy for me, you ungrateful SOB."

"Fuck you."

"Fuck me? I pulled you into this investigation because I thought it was the least I could do after Rusty made his recommendation. But you've done nothing but try to undermine my authority since the day we got started."

"Yeah? How many times did you have to suck Patterson's dick to get your little promotion?"

And there it was, the old standard, trotted out fifteen years into the twenty-first century. How did humankind manage to produce these unimaginative assholes on such a regular basis?

To his credit, Linkenfeld seemed more disgusted by the remark than Kate was. "Jesus, Bob, what the hell is wrong with you?"

She jabbed a finger toward MacLean. "You can say whatever you want—insult me, call me a bitch, a cunt—I'm pretty much bullet proof at this point. But just know this: I don't expect *any* of us to be perfect, and none of us ever will be. But if you can't handle a basic search and show me even a shred of humility when you're called out about it, then you don't belong on my team or this squad."

MacLean's face fell. "What the hell are you saying?"

"That as of now, you and Linkenfeld are no longer partners. You'll be navigating a desk in Traffic while I make the recommendation to Captain Ebersol that you be transferred out of East Division. You're done, Bob. Now pack your things and get the hell out of my squad room."

She snatched the bear and phone from the table, then turned on her heels and flung the door open, emerging from the break room to dead silence. The detectives at their desks did their best to avoid eye contact as she threaded her way past them toward her office. The walls in the building had always been thin and it was obvious that the shouting hadn't gone unnoticed.

Kate had no idea how many of these people supported her decision, although a couple of the females were smiling. She figured the least she had done was send a message loud and clear that she didn't suffer fools—or asshats—gladly.

There was, to coin a phrase, a new sheriff in town.

17

HER EX-HUSBAND WAS WAITING FOR HER in her office.

Kate had no interest in getting into another confrontation with him, so she took the civil route this time and kept it low key. "How long have you been in here?"

Dan stood at the window behind her desk, looking out at the parking lot and the expanse of the city beyond. You could almost see a sliver of the Pacific from here, and back when her promotion was announced, Kate had joked that she'd be inheriting Rusty's ocean front property.

"Not long," he said quietly. "I left the squad room when all the shouting started."

Normally Kate would have gotten her back up over a remark like this but she suddenly felt deflated. She sank into a chair in front of her desk and sighed. "They despise me, Danny. They all hate me."

Despite the walls she had built since the divorce, she still felt she could be open and honest with him. Sometimes brutally, if their exchange in the parking lot was any indication.

He turned. "It isn't hate, it's envy. Crabs in a bucket syndrome. They see you ascending and want to pull you back in." He smiled now, the picture of benevolence. "But once you get your rhythm, Katie, I have no doubt you'll be as popular as Rusty was."

She snorted. "I'll bet that wasn't easy to say."

"I'm serious."

She could see that he was and nodded. "Maybe so, but nobody'll ever be as popular as Rusty. Which is something I'll never quite understand. I mean, he's a great guy, but he was a PR man, not an investigator."

"He was popular because he never challenged anyone. He gave

people what they wanted—quick, easy to digest solutions and a record number of arrests. It didn't matter that he rarely did the actual work. We're a society that celebrates personality over substance. Even in the workplace."

Kate smiled. "Thanks. You didn't need to do that."

"Do what?"

"Try to make me feel better. Especially after how I treated you this morning."

"You react, Katie. That's how you're built. But I'm not going to stand here and pretend I'm some innocent victim. I'm not proud of what I did to you. I could have handled it a lot better."

She felt her hackles rise and raised a hand. "All right, let's not get too deep into it, before I *do* react. Why don't we talk about what you're here for?"

"That suits me."

He came over and sat in the chair next to hers. When he was facing her, she noticed he looked troubled—an expression she'd seen many times over the years.

"Your boy Christopher is quite the puzzle," he said.

"So is his so-called guardian."

"He didn't respond to my attempts at verbal communication, so an initial interview was next to impossible."

She nodded. "I had the same problem last night. Is he deaf?"

"No. He clearly heard and understood me."

"Then you made more progress than I did. The only reaction I got was when I touched his hand, but it wasn't much of one. You think he's autistic?"

"Possibly, but I can't be sure without a specialized behavioral evaluation."

"Do you think he's been coached in any way? Emotionally abused?"

Dan shook his head. "I didn't get any sense of that—although, again, it's hard to say. He didn't seem intimidated by me, and he was responsive to my commands, but never in a way that led me to believe that he was the victim of any kind of learned helplessness."

"And no adverse reactions during the physical?"

"I made it clear what I was about to do and he seemed perfectly fine with it—even the more invasive components. But he wasn't overly submissive. He was merely cooperating as any patient would."

"And he never said a word?"

"We'll get to that in a moment."

This was a curious reply, but Dan had his own way of sharing information and she decided it was best to give him room. "What about sexual or physical abuse?"

He shook his head. "Nothing recently."

"What do you mean?"

"There's no sign of trauma to the anus or perineum, no bruising or scarring of the scrotum or penis, no evidence of bite marks, nothing to suggest to me that, barring his obvious physical problems, he's anything other than a healthy young boy."

The echo of Weston's words startled Kate. "And you know this definitively?"

"No, of course not. That's only my best guess based on a preliminary exam. But with the child unable to communicate verbally, a definitive finding is unlikely."

Kate paused. "What do you mean *unable* to communicate? Is he mute?"

"In a sense, yes. He's certainly capable of vocalizing, but he'll never be normal in that regard."

"I don't understand. What are you not telling me?"

"That there's a very pronounced physical reason for his mutism. The only real sign of abuse I could find."

"Are you talking brain damage?"

"No, the injury—if you can call it that—was sustained when he was much younger, probably a good three or more years ago. And despite the healing, it's obvious it was delivered in the most brutal fashion imaginable. In fact, I'd say it's a miracle he's as well-adjusted as he seems to be."

Kate suddenly realized she was leaning forward. She thought she might know where this was headed, but the idea was too horrifying to contemplate.

"Jesus Christ, Danny, what the hell happened to him?"

It was only then that she noticed that Dan had paled slightly. He was normally a bit detached about his cases, but this one had clearly gotten to him.

"Someone mutilated that child deliberately," he said. "Somebody cut out his tongue."

PART TWO

"I will watch my ways and keep my tongue from sin; I will put a muzzle on my mouth while in the presence of the wicked."

~Psalm 39:1

18

SHE DIDN'T WANT TO PUT him in an interview room. They were small and claustrophobic and smelled of sweat, stale coffee, and (with the possible exception of the one Weston currently occupied) a hint of desperation.

True, Christopher's surroundings probably mattered less to him than your average eleven-year-old, but considering the circumstances, Kate wanted him as comfortable as possible. So she asked Dan to bring him to her office.

While Dan was gone, she took out her cell phone, crossed to the window facing the squad room and peeked through the blinds, hoping to gauge the temperature out there.

She saw Linkenfeld logging some computer time, but his ex-partner was nowhere to be seen. MacLean had undoubtedly started making phone calls the moment she left them and was now meeting with Captain Ebersol, or a union rep, in hopes of finding a way to stay at East Division. She expected nothing less from a man who had fought hard for this job, and knew all too well that their confrontation in the break room was merely the opening salvo in what was likely to be an all-out war.

But none of that mattered at the moment. Uppermost in her mind right now was her father's phone call this morning, and the words that had come back to haunt her.

You didn't find any missing tongues, did you?

Well, yes, Mitch. Apparently I have.

While Kate was the first to admit that coincidences do happen, she wondered if this was more than that. Was it possible that this boy was connected to a mass murder in Tacoma, Washington? The mutilation he'd suffered had happened years ago, but the fact that he was running around with a man who was a victim—and suspect—of a similar crime raised a red flag so big and so bright that Kate could barely see past it.

She looked down at her cell phone, found the number she had called less than an hour ago and hoped the man she'd talked to was still available.

The line rang three times before it was picked up. "Stokes County District Attorney's Office. How may I direct your call?"

"Lieutenant Kate Messenger for Charles Dillman."

"Just a moment, please, I'll see if he's available."

She waited that moment, then the line came alive with a cool but gentle North Carolina drawl. "Well now, that was mighty quick. You get our boy to confess?"

Kate huffed. "Getting him to do much of anything is a minor miracle."

"Don't I know it. Weston's got a mind of his own. So what can I do for you this time?"

"I need to know something about the condition of the Weston family bodies. Something that wasn't mentioned in the news accounts."

"Something Weston told you?"

"No, but the coincidences are piling up and I don't like it."

"Well don't keep me in suspense."

"The victims tongues," she said. "Did Anna Weston and her daughters have their tongues cut out?"

There was a long silence. Too long.

"Mr. Dillman?"

"Are you saying that *your* victims had their tongues cut out?"

"No. They were brutalized but not like that. I don't think there's any connection between the two cases at all, other than Weston's presence at my crime scene."

"Then I don't understand. If there's no connection and Weston didn't say anything, where are you getting this from?"

"You haven't answered my question."

He was silent again. Then he said, "The answer is yes. They all had their tongues cut out with what our forensics people believe was a three-quarter-inch bimetal bandsaw blade—the kind you find in saw mills the world over." He paused. "Weston owned a saw mill. One of the biggest in Stokes County."

Kate felt a chill run through her. "Did you find the blade?"

"Not a sign of it anywhere. But we withheld all these details from the press, redacted it from the forensic files. And since Weston claimed to have found the bodies, it seemed reasonable that he might know about the tongue cutting, but we made a point of never mentioning the specific weapon involved, in hopes he'd slip up in one of the interviews. He never did."

"He doesn't strike me as a guy who slips up very often."

"All it takes is once," Dillman said. "Are you sure there's no connection between these two crimes?"

"I'm sure. We already have a person of interest. It may be a dead end, but my gut tells me it isn't."

"Then I still don't understand. How do you know about the tongues?"

Kate crossed to her desk. "Because of a case up in Tacoma three months ago you might not have heard about if you weren't watching the bulletins. I don't know if it involves bandsaw blades, but it's my understanding from an inside source that the victims also had their tongues removed."

She opened Weston's file, took out the sketch book, and began flipping through the pages, studying the drawings.

Damn, they were good.

"Now that *is* interesting," Dillman said. "But I'm still a little confused. If your case isn't connected, what on earth compelled you to ask about our victims' tongues?"

Kate spotted a drawing that grabbed her attention and stopped on the page. "You remember the boy I mentioned? The blind one, who's traveling with him?"

"Oh, yes I do. Weston never struck me as a kiddie diddler, but I suppose a man who's capable of murdering his entire family is capable of just about anything."

"Well, my guy from CPS tells me the boy's also had his tongue cut out."

Kate was greeted with the longest silence yet, and she had a feeling the cool, unflappable man she'd been dealing with up until now had just had his foundation rocked. She looked down at the drawing in front of her and saw a detailed sketch of a wooden post with a sign that read WELCOME TO TACOMA.

"What's strange," she went on, "is that it looks as if the boy was hurt several years before the Weston murders. So I can't quite figure out how he fits in."

When Dillman found his voice, he said, "I can see why you're concerned about coincidences. It's obvious I've got a bit of work ahead of me."

She studied the sketch. "We both do."

"I take it you haven't identified this boy?"

"Not yet. But I'm having him brought up for an interview, and if we can find a way to communicate, I'm hoping I can fill in some missing details."

"And I'm hoping you're right," Dillman said. "Let me know how it goes."

Kate told him she would and was about to hang up when Dillman stopped her.

"When you talk to Weston again, mention those tongues and see if you can get him to bring up that bandsaw blade. I want to nail this guy something bad."

Maybe a little too bad, Kate thought, then bid him goodbye and hung up.

19

WHILE SHE WAITED FOR DAN to return with Christopher, Kate got on her phone again and called Curt Clark, one of the juniors she'd sent to chase down Chucho Soriano. According to Soriano's file, his last known address was a walk-up apartment building in an area of West Santa Flora that wasn't known for its easygoing lifestyle. It didn't quite qualify as a slum, but you wouldn't want to be strolling around there at midnight.

Even noon was iffy.

"You having any luck?" she asked Clark.

"The LKA was a bust. But the woman next door used to hang with Soriano sometimes and says he's got a brother lives near the Greyhound station, so we're headed that way."

"What's the brother's name?"

"Emilio. Supposedly some kind of computer geek, designs porn websites. Soriano showed a couple to the neighbor one time and told her she should think about modeling."

"Classy," Kate said.

Had he done the same to Bree Branford?

"It's been a few months since he left the location, so there's no guarantee he'll be at Emilio's."

The fear, of course, was that Soriano had skipped town altogether. And if that was the case, they'd have to cast a wide net and maybe even get the press involved—which Kate would rather avoid.

"If he isn't there, put some pressure on the brother. We need to find this guy."

"How much pressure?"

"Use your best judgment," she said, "but don't get carried away."

"You got it, lieutenant. We'll be in touch."

·

A moment later, the door opened and Dan escorted Christopher inside and sat him in the same chair Kate had occupied earlier. He looked smaller than she remembered, and a bit forlorn, reminding her of one of those *Save the Children* commercials full of kids with soulful, hungry stares.

Except that wasn't quite right, was it?

This particular kid had a stare as vacant as a dormant computer screen, and gave no indication whether he wanted to be saved or simply left alone. His gaze was fixed on the window behind her desk as he quietly rocked, and she wondered what he saw.

Light and dark? Indistinct shapes? Nothing at all?

"I assume you want me to stay," Dan said.

"Absolutely."

He nodded and perched on the edge of her desk as Kate moved around it to the chair next to Christopher.

As she sat, Dan made a gesture with his hand as if to say, *be gentle,* which—as he well knew—wasn't a state of being that came naturally to Kate. She thought of the most gentle person she'd ever known and channeled the spirit of her mother.

"Good morning, Christopher. I'm Kate. I came to your motel room last night, remember?"

The boy rocked, giving no indication she existed.

"Dr. Brennan says you were very cooperative during your check-up this morning, so I know you can hear me. Can you nod for me? Show me you're listening?"

Still nothing. She may as well have been talking to an animatronic robot.

She looked up at Dan.

"Give him time," he said. "Let him warm up to you."

Kate nodded and was about to try again when a thought struck her. Getting to her feet, she crossed to a corner of her office where she had stowed the boy's suitcase. She unlatched it and pulled it open, taking out the small pink photo album with the name *Lucy* scrawled across it.

She went back to her chair, sat down, and placed a hand on Christopher's knee. He flinched again—just as he had last night—

but he still didn't acknowledge her presence.

"I've got something of yours, and I'm thinking you may want it." She took hold of his hand and placed the album on his palm. "I'll bet you've been missing this."

His reaction was swift. He stopped rocking, grabbed hold of it with both hands and smiled, pulling it to his chest. Then he brought it up to his nose and breathed it in as if it gave him life.

And in a way, it had.

"I'm sure Dr. Brennan told you there's nothing to be afraid of, but I need you to listen to me like you did to him. Can you do that? Can you listen?"

She half expected him to ignore her again, but he lowered the album and nodded.

Relieved, Kate smiled. "Good. That's really good." She glanced at Dan, who gave her a thumbs up. "Now I'm going ask to you some questions. And since I know this is hard for you, all you have to do is nod your head or shake it. Yes or no. Can you do that for me?"

Another delay, then another nod.

"Excellent," she said. "I know all this must be very confusing for you, but—"

He shook his head suddenly and Kate paused.

"Are you saying it *isn't* confusing?"

He nodded.

"Then you know why you're here?"

He nodded again and she again looked at Dan. "What did you tell him?"

"I just assured him he wasn't in any kind of trouble and that we were only doing what we felt was best for him."

She turned. "Do you understand that, Christopher? That we're only trying to do what's best for you?"

He nodded. And though she couldn't explain the near trancelike states until now, she suspected he was neither autistic nor mentally challenged.

He was smart. And very aware.

He knew exactly what was going on.

"Have you been through something like this before?"

Another nod.

"With Mr. Weston? Have the two of you been in trouble with the police?"

This time he shook his head, but then he did something that startled Kate.

Leaning forward slightly, he opened his mouth and wiggled the pink stub of his tongue at her. The sight was both horrifying and heartbreaking and she knew immediately what he was trying to say.

"You spent time with the police after you were hurt."

He nodded, then closed his mouth and sat upright. Message sent.

She paused. "Who hurt you, Christopher? Was it Mr. Weston?"

He shook his head, vigorously this time, but she wasn't all that surprised. She'd already come to this conclusion herself. If Dan was right about the timing of the injury, Weston would've had to have done it a couple of years before he slaughtered his own family—which made little sense. And while she had humored Dillman in his belief that Weston was a murderer, her gut told her he was wrong. Sure, the man was infuriating and evasive and wired a little differently than your average human being, and yes, that sketch on her desk indicated that they'd been to Tacoma, but the more she considered it, the less she was willing to tag him with that particular label.

"Can we talk about what happened to you, Christopher? About how you got hurt?"

The boy hesitated, and she knew this had to be difficult for him.

"Would you rather we talk about Mr. Weston instead? Maybe you can help me understand why the two of you were at my crime —"

The boy reached forward and pressed his fingers to her lips.

With another vigorous shake of his head, he swiveled in Dan's direction, then took his hand from her mouth and made a quick gesture, bringing his fingers down to touch his thumb as if he were closing the mouth of a sock puppet.

Kate had no idea what this meant, but Dan's expression said that he did. "He's using sign language. He wants me to leave."

Kate frowned. "But he's blind. How does he know sign language?"

"He's also speech-impaired, so someone must have taught it to him."

Kate thought about the labor intensive task of teaching sign language to a boy who couldn't see, but didn't pursue any of the questions this brought to mind. Instead she simply said, "Is that what you mean, Christopher? You want Dr. Brennan to leave?"

He nodded and made the gesture again.

"But if he leaves and you use sign language, I won't be able to understand what you're—"

He gestured a third time, making it clear that he wouldn't take no for an answer.

Kate didn't know why this was so important to him, but she wasn't sure sending Dan away was a good idea. Allowing yourself to be left alone with a witness or a suspect was a recipe for disaster. All kinds of claims could be made that might derail your career.

Especially by eleven-year-old boys.

And after their stunt at the Branford house last night, Kate didn't know if she could trust Christopher any more than she trusted Weston. There might be another surprise waiting for her the moment Dan stepped out of the room.

"I know what you're thinking," Dan said, "but I doubt it's anything to be concerned about. And if my absence will help our young friend here open up even more, then it's worth the risk."

Easy for you to say, Kate thought.

But he was right. Curiosity was not the only thing driving her now. She wanted to get to the truth.

"All right," she said. "But don't go too far."

Dan stood up, patted Christopher's shoulder and headed for the door. "I'll be right outside if you need me."

"Thanks," she said, then watched him exit and close the door behind him.

As she turned to face Christopher again, she was struck by the thought that something about him had changed—and abruptly at that. He sat in the same position, his milky eyes fixed in her direction, but there was a sudden stillness to him that hadn't been evident before.

He wasn't ignoring her like before. Just the opposite, in fact. He was very much present in the room, rendered immobile by a kind of fixed concentration, as if he were centering all of his focus outward.

Toward *her.*

She was about to ask him if he was okay, when a voice inside her head—a voice that was clearly not hers—said:

Etak, su fo eno er'uoy.

20

KATE BLINKED, SUCKED IN A breath, and drew back as if she'd been confronted by a perp with a weapon. For a moment she thought Christopher had spoken aloud, but she knew that was impossible.

She'd *seen* why it was impossible.

Yako, s'ti. Diarfa eb t'nod.

There it was again—the same voice she'd heard last night, yet stronger. More invasive. Not some nebulous radio transmission, but clear and clean as if he were whispering directly in her ear.

But this time Kate couldn't blame stress or anxiety or sleep deprivation. This time she knew that what she was hearing was as real as the chair she sat in. The boy was speaking to her with his *mind*, for Christ's sake, projecting his thoughts directly into her.

Em dnatsrednu uoy od?

Kate couldn't move. Didn't *want* to move. Sat transfixed as he continued to speak.

Dnatsrednu uoy ekam ot deen i.

And that language. Where had she heard it before? It sounded so oddly familiar. As if... As if...

As if he were speaking backwards.

Yes. That was it.

She thought of the many times she had rewound surveillance tapes on one of those old reel-to-reels, back when the department was still using equipment that had been purchased during the Nixon administration. She'd put a finger to a reel to drag the tape across the playhead, rewinding it slowly, trying to isolate a particular phrase. The sound coming from Christopher had the same strange, musical cadence and she assumed that somewhere in the transition from his brain to *hers*, the signal had gotten...

Jesus. What was she thinking?

She was acting as if this was normal. As if it was just another interview with a witness.

She knew she should have been blown away, or writing it off as some kind of parlor trick, but this was no trick, and in an odd sort of way, it *did* feel normal.

Was she dreaming?

This *was* real, wasn't it?

As if he had been reading her thoughts, Christopher furrowed his brow, concentrating harder, then spoke again. And Kate wasn't sure why, but this time he managed to get the words through to her unscrambled:

Do you... understand me?

She blinked at him, barely able to speak, but slowly nodded. "... Yes."

I would've talked to you at the motel last night... but those policemen were there. I need you to see something, Kate. That's why I told Doctor Brennan to leave.

He sounded young, but there was a maturity to his tone that surprised Kate. He was certainly well beyond any eleven-year-old she'd ever encountered. But then he wasn't your average eleven-year-old, was he?

She swallowed, not sure what to do with herself. Still not completely convinced she hadn't taken a dive into a shallow pool and smacked her head.

Just talk to me like you did before. That's how Noah does it.

Kate nodded again and still had trouble finding her voice. "Promise me I'm not going crazy. Because I've gotta tell you, I'm on the fence right now."

You aren't crazy.

"But how is this even possible? How are you doing this?"

Noah thinks I was born this way. He thinks we both were.

Was that why Weston hadn't been concerned about Christopher? Had they been in psychic contact ever since they were separated?

"So why share it with *me*?" she asked. "Is it because I'm the one who came to the house last night?"

You came there because I wanted you to.

"What are you talking about?"

You didn't know it then, but I was calling to you.

Kate stared at him. Could that be possible?

She thought back to last night and how she'd been driving around, trying to clear her head after the unpleasant encounter with her father. She had wanted to head home but found herself driving to the crime scene.

Had something drawn her there?

We didn't go to that house because of the people who were killed there. We went there because of you.

"Me?"

Noah doesn't know that yet, which is why he told me to play that trick on you last night. I went along because I could see you weren't ready to talk to me. Not then.

Not now either, Kate thought. She wasn't sure she'd ever be ready.

"Okay, but why me?"

Because you're one of us, Kate.

"One of us? What does that mean?"

You were born with the gift, too.

She shook her head. "That's ridiculous."

Think about the things you know. The things you feel that others don't. The things you find that others pass by.

"It's called intuition," she said. "A lot of people are like that."

But most of them can't hear me. Most of them would think you're talking to yourself right now.

Kate thought about this.

Was she talking to herself?

No, I told you this is real. And there's something else we share.

"Which is?"

It's easier if I show you.

"What do you mean? Show me what?"

He took the pink photo album from his lap and held it out to her.

You knew this was important to me. You knew it would bring me out of the haze.

"Haze?"

It's where I go sometimes. But something told you to bring this photo book to me. Because it's important to both of us.

"I don't understand."

It's like Noah's sketch pad. A way of sharing the pictures.

Kate looked at his outstretched hand and studied the album dubiously. "I already looked in there. There's nothing to see."

He gestured for her to take hold of it.

I'll help you. But when the pictures come, they'll come fast and you may not like it. So you have to be ready.

Kate hesitated. Ready for what?

But she was on the hook now and there was no going back. She reached out and took the album from him, turning it in her hands.

Go ahead and open it.

She did as she was told, already knowing what was inside, expecting to see that canned portrait of some anonymous, telegenic family. But to her surprise the album was filled with photographs now, snapshots of a little girl, taken over the course of several years.

Lucy?

But before she could even register surprise, the photos began to shift and change in front of her eyes, morphing into images she had seen before, images that had lingered in her mind ever since she sought them out in the Open Unsolved storage room.

Pictures of a woman's battered body, found between two Dumpsters in the alley behind the Sandy Point Mall.

Crime scene photos.

Her *mother's* crime scene photos....

21

KATE WANTED TO FLEE, WANTED to jump up and run from the room and keep running until she was out of breath and her feet were sore. Until she had put as much distance as she possibly could between herself and these photographs and this strange little boy.

But before she could think beyond this simple impulse, she felt herself being pulled toward the photo album, invisible hands wrapping around her and urging her forward. Then suddenly she was falling, flailing, tumbling through darkness as images of her mother's twisted corpse enveloped and swirled around her, pulling her deeper and deeper into the vortex.

Then all at once they were gone and she was standing.

But not in her office.

It was night and chilly and she stood at the mouth of a dark alley, looking toward a pool of incandescent light that came from a bulb over a blue metal door. Just past the door were two Dumpsters, overflowing with cardboard boxes and black plastic bags.

Hold on, now. What was happening to her? Where was she?

But she already knew the answer.

How could she *not* know?

She was standing in the alley behind the Sandy Point Mall. But it wasn't the alley you'd find there today, the walls and adjoining brick fence covered with a decade's worth of graffiti. This was the alley of many years past, the alley from the photographs, where her mother's body had been found.

Drawing in a sharp breath, Kate shifted her gaze to the space between the two Dumpsters and saw a dark shape lying on the asphalt.

Oh, Jesus. Oh, God...

She didn't want to move, but found herself stepping forward anyway, walking toward that dark shape as she unhooked the flashlight from her belt.

She glanced down at her hand and realized with dismay that it wasn't *her* hand she was looking at. It was a man's hand—big and sinewy and covered with tufts of dark hair. And the clothes she wore were not *her* clothes, but a uniform—a security guard's uniform.

The placard on her chest read M. BONNER, and she recognized that name from her mother's murder file. Michael Bonner was the guard who had been working the mall that night twenty years ago and had discovered Cassandra Messenger's body.

It was at this point that Kate decided that she was definitely dreaming. Not just this moment of insanity, but the entire day. The call from her father, the fight with Dan, the confrontations with Bob MacLean and Noah Weston, the phone calls with Dillman, the encounter with a boy who spoke to her with his mind and may or may not have been the victim of a psychopath...

What Kate had only moments ago thought was real and even normal was clearly very far from that. She was in the middle of an epic nightmare and any moment now she'd wake up and either be at home in bed or strapped to a gurney in a padded room.

She wanted to flee again, but realized that wasn't possible because she wasn't in control of this body. The guy who owned it, way back in 1995, was still moving forward, completely unaware that the daughter of the woman he was about to find was on an unofficial ridealong.

They slowed as they approached, then crouched together just feet from the body, and shone the flashlight beam across it.

Kate sucked in another sharp breath at the sight of the glassy eyes, the gaping mouth, the purple and black bruises darkening the skin. If she hadn't seen the crime scene photos, she wouldn't even know this was her mother.

The mother she remembered was soft and lovely and always warm and kind and attentive. But the beating she had suffered seemed to have taken all of that away from her, leaving only this soulless shell behind. A soulless shell that...

Wait now.

What was Bonner doing?

He had gotten up and moved closer to the body and was now leaning toward it. He placed the flashlight on the ground, positioning it to shine its beam across her mother's face, then reached forward with his left hand and placed his palm over her eyes.

When it came away, they were closed.

This was a sweet enough gesture, but didn't Bonner realize he was tampering with a crime scene? Sure, he was only a security guard, but he had to know that you never, under any circumstances, touch the...

Oh, Jesus.

Now he was lowering his left hand—*their* left hand—to her mother's open mouth, sticking a finger inside.

What the *fuck* was he doing?

Then the thumb went in and to Kate's utter astonishment, he grabbed hold of her mother's tongue as his right hand went to his belt and reappeared carrying a utility knife. And it was only then that Kate noticed a mark on his inner wrist, peeking out from under his shirt cuff:

A crude black circle with a dot in the center, like the single ring of a target with a bullseye. The same tattoo—the same wrist, in fact—she'd seen in Weston's sketchpad.

Bonner now flicked the utility knife open, exposing steel, and lowered it toward her mother's mouth.

Oh, Jesus. Oh, God...

Kate felt sick and horrified and outraged all at once, watching him—*feeling* him—pull on that tongue until he'd exposed enough lingual membrane to make room for the blade. And just as he was about to cut her—to *mutilate* her—a voice called out from behind him:

"Hey, Mickey, what the hell is taking you so..."

The voice trickled to a halt as Bonner—and Kate—quickly let go, stowed the utility knife, and spun around to find another security guard standing at the mouth of the alley, his eyes wide with disbelief.

"Jesus H. Christ..."

"I was just checking her vitals," Bonner said in a deep voice, "and it looks like we've got a DB on our hands."

As Kate inwardly began to wretch, she found herself falling again, tumbling forward, plunging into a swirling, chaotic darkness, shedding Bonner's body like an old skin....

And a moment later she opened her eyes and was back in her office, seated next to Christopher, the pink photo album in her hands, its plastic pages empty except for a single canned photograph of a smiling, anonymous family.

Without a word, she dropped it to the floor and bolted across the room.

22

BY THE TIME SHE GOT INTO the restroom, she couldn't remember what she'd said to Dan as she flew past him.

"Keep an eye on him" or something along those lines—meaning Christopher, of course. Although she had a feeling the boy was perfectly capable of taking care of himself. He'd certainly done a number on her.

Dan had called out to her, asking if she was okay, but she'd ignored him and come straight here. Now she slammed her way into a stall, leaned toward the toilet bowl and let fly, relieving herself of about a gallon of coffee and some of last night's dinner.

When she was done, she grabbed a wad of toilet paper, wiped her mouth and felt her legs go weak. She sank to the floor, leaned back against the booth wall, and before she knew it she was crying. Not loud, but there were enough tears streaming down her cheeks to require another wad of toilet paper.

Kate hated crying. Had hated it ever since she cried herself to sleep every night for two weeks after her mother's murder. It was supposed to bring you relief, but all she'd felt was exhaustion and sadness and defeat. And in the years since, she had done her best to turn off that part of her brain, to never allow sentiment to take hold of her again.

To control her.

That was what Kate thrived on. Control. And losing it in her office like that, seeing what she was forced to see, *being* there in that alleyway with the man who had surely killed her mother, had left her feeling helpless and a little scared. Especially now that Christopher's words made sense to her.

Because you're one of us.

She was a victim. Like Christopher. And Weston. And that family up in Tacoma. It was clear to her that the guard in that alleyway, the man who claimed to have found her mother's body, had done much more than that. He was the same man who had victimized them all.

Because you're one of us.

Bonner may have failed to cut out her mother's tongue, but only by chance. After spending those few moments inside his body, seeing what he saw, feeling what he felt, Kate knew that the tongue-cutting gave him some kind of release. Brought him the relief that crying was supposed to give her.

Had her mother been the first of his victims? The beginning of a two decade-long killing spree?

She needed to get down to the file room, get hold of the murder book and find Bonner's statement. Find out as much as she could about the guy.

Where had he gone after his interview with the police?

And where was he now?

Wiping the last of her tears, she climbed to her feet and was headed out of the booth when she heard the restroom door fly open and someone said, "Hey, Messenger, you okay in here?"

She recognized that voice immediately.

Rusty Patterson.

23

SHE CAME OUT OF THE STALL and saw Rusty standing just inside the doorway in jeans and plaid shirt, a craggy Tommy Lee Jones doppelgänger with just a touch of Keith Carradine thrown in for good measure. And despite herself, she burst into tears again.

He came forward and wrapped his arms around her and in that moment she realized just how much she missed him. For all her criticism of his investigatory skills, she admired his effortless charm and uncanny ability to get people to do things for him. *She* had been one of those people, and had never once felt used or abused. She didn't really want his job. She wanted *him* to want his job and to stay where he belonged.

Rusty was still a young man—fifty-eight, if her count was right— and she'd never understood why he'd been so anxious to retire.

He patted her back and said, "One of those days, huh?"

She pulled away from him and wiped at her tears with her sleeve. "You wouldn't believe me if I told you."

"I know the feeling. But this may be a first. I don't think I've ever seen you reduced to tears."

"Blame it on the divorce and the new job," she said, avoiding any mention of the Tilt-a-Whirl ride she'd just taken. "I'm still trying to adjust."

He nodded. "That's understandable. And I probably should've warned you that the job wouldn't be easy. The trick is to make it look that way."

She smiled now. "You're definitely the master of that. When did you get back in town?"

"Couple days ago. Bangkok was too damn hot. Heard I missed a big one up in Oak Grove while I was gone."

Kate nodded. "Five dead, along with the family dog."

He paused, looking serious. "I also heard from Bob MacLean. Just got off the phone with him, in fact."

Kate stiffened. "Why am I not surprised?"

"He's a good man, Kate. You gotta give *him* time to adjust, too."

Kate couldn't believe this. The war was already starting. And it was the last thing she needed right now. "Is that why you're here? To beg me to give Bob his job back?"

"I'm not big on begging," he said.

"Yeah, but you've always been the peacekeeper. Can't stand it when the kids fight. Did he tell you what he missed at our crime scene?"

Rusty shrugged. "He mentioned one of the vics hid a cell phone, but come on, Kate, we've all made those kinds of mistakes at one time or a—"

"Did he tell you what was on that phone?"

"No, he didn't, but—"

"It was a major lead, Rusty. A possible suspect. A guy we could've pulled in here days ago if Bob had done his job." She sighed. "But that isn't why I brought the hammer down. Bob isn't *interested* in adjusting. His world centers around what's best for Bob MacLean, and everyone else can go screw themselves. I don't need someone like that on my squad."

Rusty studied her a moment. "Your squad. I've gotta admit it's a little strange hearing someone else say that."

"You can always have it back," she said. "You didn't have to retire."

He shook his head. "I promised myself a long time ago I'd travel the world before I hit sixty and that deadline's approaching faster than I'd like. Bangkok was just the start. I plan to fly to Hamburg next, then head on to Amsterdam from there."

Kate raised a brow. "You've never struck me as the globetrotting type."

He shrugged. "I'm mostly trying to get away from the ex-wives. They both seem to think they're still married to me."

They laughed, relieving the tension, but then Kate got serious again, her little trip into the Twilight Zone still lingering in her brain.

How could it not be?

"While you're here," she said, "I need to ask you about something. Can I buy you a cup of coffee?"

"I think I can make the time."

24

KATE WANTED TO AVOID THE employee break room, so they went to the vending machine in the hallway. She dropped some coins, waited for the cup to fill, then handed it to Rusty, who took one sip and promptly deposited it in a nearby trash can.

"Now I know why I never bought that pig's wash. Why don't we go up to the chapel so I can catch a smoke instead?"

Kate thought about Christopher still waiting in her office, but figured Dan could stay with him for awhile. They hit the stairwell and wound their way up three flights of stairs to the roof of the building, which everyone in the department called the chapel. It was empty up here, giving them privacy, along with a much better view of the city and the Pacific beyond.

Kate hadn't been outside in hours and the sun felt good on her face.

As Rusty dug a pack of Winstons from his shirt pocket and lit one up, she said, "What do you know about my mother's murder?"

Rusty paused and blew out smoke. "Is *that* what the tears were about?"

"You were with the department when it happened."

"I was. But I was junior at the time."

"Tell me what you know."

Rusty contemplated the tip of his cigarette, flicked away some ash. "What I know is next to nothing. It wasn't my case and I never even went to the crime scene."

"Do you know anything about the witnesses?"

"Just that there were two. Couple of security guards. My partner and I transported one of them, brought him in from his apartment for a follow-up interview. That was my only involvement."

"Which security guard? What was his name?"

"Hell, I don't remember. Bonham. Donner. Something like that. The guy who found her. Kate, I understand your curiosity, but are you sure you wanna be opening this particular wound?"

"What can you tell me about him? What kind of guy was he?"

Rusty took a drag and shrugged. "He didn't talk much. And he was big. I remember thinking that when we escorted him to the cruiser. Twenty-two, three, somewhere around there. Of course, I could be confusing him with someone else. They all blend together after awhile."

"Any idea what happened to him after the follow-up?"

"Where are you going with this? You thinking this guy might be good for your mom's murder?"

"It's a possibility."

"And what led you to this conclusion?"

"You wouldn't believe me if I told you."

"You'd be surprised what I might believe. I've pretty much seen it all."

"It's nothing. Just me hypothesizing. Wondering how long the guy had been working at Sandy Point when he found her body and how long he stuck around afterwards."

Rusty shrugged. "Wish I could help you, but I can't. If I'm remembering right, the lead investigator on the case was Harry Metzler, but he's been dead for years. I'm guessing he followed standard protocol, looked into both guards and didn't find any ties to your mother. You talk to your dad about this?"

"Not a chance. The subject's off limits with him."

"Did you check the file?"

"That's my next stop. What about your partner? The one who went with you. Is he still around?"

Rusty shook his head. "Name was Abernathy. Good man, but he had his share of problems. Started acting up shortly after that."

"In what way?"

"He got busted for forcibly sodomizing a hooker and wound up eating his own gun."

"Jesus," Kate said.

Rusty took another long drag. "That's the problem with this job. You stick around long enough, see the things we see, it's like a virus. Some people have a natural immunity and some people get eaten alive." He dropped the half smoked cigarette to the rooftop, stamped it out and smiled. "And some people buy a plane ticket to Amsterdam."

25

WESTON WAS DOZING IN HIS CHAIR when the door opened and Lieutenant Messenger brought Christopher into the interview room.

This was a surprise. What was she planning now?

But as he shook himself alert, he noted almost immediately that the lieutenant's demeanor had softened somewhat.

"I'm cutting you loose," she said. "Both of you."

Even more of a surprise. "What?"

She came over to unlock his cuffs and he saw a vague but discernible uneasiness in her eyes, as if she hadn't quite found her footing after a bad spill. She seemed unsure of herself but was trying to hide it.

"What changed your mind?" he asked.

"I don't see any point in holding you anymore. You were right. The doctor who examined Christopher says there's no evidence he's been mistreated—not lately, anyway—and I'm willing to cut you some slack on the trespassing and obstruction beefs."

She unhooked him and Weston rubbed his wrists, wondering what was going on here. An hour ago she had practically called him a murderer and child molester.

"What are you not telling me?"

She paused, and in that moment seemed to regain some of her balance. "There's a condition to your release."

Ah. So there it was. "Which is?"

"You let me buy you some lunch."

"What?"

"I'm sure Christopher's hungry, and you and I have a lot to talk about."

This didn't make any sense. What could they possibly have to talk about that hadn't already been discussed? Unless...

He looked at Christopher. "What did you tell her?"

"It was more show than tell," she said.

Weston understood what that meant, and it explained her initial uneasiness. He'd felt the same way the first time the boy had opened up to him.

But why? Why would he tell her anything? They had talked about this numerous times, and had agreed it was best to keep a low profile. Sharing his gift with a stranger—a stranger who was a cop no less—was dangerous business.

Weston waited for Chris to chime in, but got nothing from him. He was gone, in the haze, wandering in whatever playground waited for him there.

"What did he show you?"

"That's what we need to talk about."

"And if I refuse?"

She held up the cuffs. "Forty-eight hours, remember?"

26

HE ORDERED CHRISTOPHER A BOWL of chili—one of his favorites—but it was doubtful he'd even touch it. They sat at a table at the back of a small diner across from the police department, the boy rocking quietly and getting more than a few stares.

When they had first stepped inside, Weston had looked around, saw tables full of police officers and wondered if this place was the best choice to be having this particular conversation. If the lieutenant wanted to talk about the things Chris had shown her, it might've been wise to find someplace a little more private.

But she didn't look concerned. Every bit of her trepidation had vanished and her focus seemed to be limited to the three of them. And after they finished ordering (hers a terse demand for black coffee), she pulled Weston's sketchpad out of her handbag and placed it on the table.

"Explain this to me."

"Didn't we already have this discussion?"

"I wouldn't characterize anything we've had as a discussion. So please do me a favor and quit avoiding my questions."

"Seems to me you've already answered a lot of them yourself." He nodded to the boy. "With Christopher's help, of course."

She tapped the sketch pad. "You told me earlier that people wouldn't envy your talent if they knew why you drew these. So why did you? Do they come from him?"

"You already know they do."

"All I know is that something happened to me today that I can't explain. Something Christopher did. And I'm just trying to figure it out."

"And what'll happen when you do?"

"I don't know," she said. "I'm in uncharted territory here."

She flipped open the sketch pad, found a specific page, then jabbed a finger at one of the drawings.

It was a sketch of the tattoo on the Beast's forearm.

"I assume this came from Christopher, too?"

"Why do you keep asking me things you already know?"

She tapped the drawing. "What does it mean?"

"It's called a circumpunct. A circle with a dot—or bindu—at its center. Its meaning could be any number of things, but one of the most common beliefs is that it represents God."

"How long ago did you draw it?"

He shrugged. "It's been a few months now."

"And where did it come from? From Christopher's memory? Because I'm assuming he was a victim of this man."

Weston stared at her. "You really don't know how this works, do you?"

"How it works?" Her eyes were a little wild. "I don't even know what *this is*. What the hell is happening?"

He watched her for a moment, almost feeling sorry for her. The first time Chris had reached out to him, he'd felt that same sense of confusion. The same disbelief. "Let me ask *you* a question instead. What exactly did Chris show you?"

She breathed deep, settled herself, and pointed to the sketch again. "A man with a tattoo just like this. Only it wasn't a photograph or a drawing."

"Then what was it?"

"I'm not sure," she said. "Like a vision or a dream. Only it felt real. Like I was stuck inside him."

"Inside Chris?"

She shook her head. "The man with the tattoo."

Weston hesitated. This was something new. "I don't get it. What are you saying?"

"Exactly what it sounds like. When Christopher did whatever it is he does, I felt as if I was trapped inside this man's body. He had just killed a woman and was about to cut out her tongue."

Weston felt a chill. All he'd ever gotten from Chris were the sketches. "Where did this happen?"

"In my office."

"No, in the vision. Where were you?"

"In an alleyway behind the Sandy Point Mall." She paused. "In nineteen ninety-five."

"*What?*"

"The woman I saw has been dead for nearly two decades."

"How do you know that?"

"Because she was my mother."

This stopped Weston cold.

The deepest he'd ever seen Christopher go was days, not years. And certainly not two decades. But if what she said was true, then her mother may have been one of the Beast's first victims.

Weston watched Christopher rock in his chair, wishing the boy would snap out of it. He thought about the last few days and Chris's insistence that they leave Reno and head for Santa Flora— even though the crime at the Branford house seemed to have nothing to do with the Beast. Then there was the near meltdown when Weston wanted to ditch the Rambler and disappear. The shouting that had nearly made his head explode.

Had Chris been planning this encounter all along? Had going to that house been nothing more than subterfuge, designed to bring about a meeting with Lieutenant Kate Messenger?

That would explain the stop they'd made before heading into Oak Grove.

"We've been in that alley, too," Weston said.

"When?"

"Yesterday afternoon. I wasn't sure why Chris wanted to go there and he wouldn't tell me."

"I know how that feels."

Weston ignored the remark. "I thought it was just a mistake. He makes them sometimes. But I can see now he had a very specific reason for going there. He must've seen something earlier that lead him to—"

Kate raised a hand. "Slow down a minute. You just told me I don't know how this works and you're right, I don't. So why don't you back up a bit and explain it to me?"

"I don't know anything about visions or dreams. That's never happened before. Not to me, at least." He patted the sketch pad. "This is as far as it's ever gotten."

"So tell me what you *do* know. Tell me about this... gathering thing."

He studied her again, still not sure he could trust her. Was this all some elaborate ruse to get him to confess to some kind of crime?

But if that were true, how could she possibly know what the boy was capable of?

How would she know any of this?

Before he could respond, the waitress came back with their order—Christopher's chili, the lieutenant's coffee, and an egg salad sandwich for Weston.

Weston hoped the smell of the chili would bring Chris out of the haze, but Chris continued to rock, oblivious to everything and everyone around him.

Weston released a long breath and turned to the lieutenant.

"This is how it works," he said.

27

"EVERY CRIME SCENE HAS A smell. A look. A trail of DNA. But I guess you know that better than I do."

Kate nodded, but said nothing. She was trying her best to hide it, but she still felt unsettled and queasy.

"What you don't know," Weston continued, "is that it also has a feel. A kind of... emotional residue."

"I don't understand," she said.

"It's like the smell of rotting garbage that lingers in a room after the trash has been taken out. When someone commits a crime, there are a lot of emotions involved. Terror. Anxiety. Anger. Surprise. Grief. A kind of chaotic stew that envelops both the victims and the perpetrator and stays behind long after they're gone." He paused, glanced at Christopher. "Apparently a lot longer than I thought."

"This sounds like something out of a movie."

"Believe me, sometimes I wish it were, but I've seen and felt its power. And if what you're telling me is true, so have you."

Kate thought about that alleyway and felt the room sway. She steadied herself. "I take it Christopher has found some way to tap into this residue?"

"Don't ask me how, but yes. What you saw him doing in the Branford living room was what he calls gathering. He soaks in whatever's still lingering in the room—the feelings and even some of the memories of the people involved."

Kate gestured to the sketchpad. "Which he sends to you."

Weston nodded. "You mentioned how talented I am, but the truth is, I can barely draw stick figures."

Kate thought he was joking but realized he wasn't. "So this is all Christopher?"

"It certainly isn't me. But when he sends me the pictures, I go into my own little trance and the drawings are waiting for me on the other side. I barely remember putting the pencil to the paper."

"So you have no control over what winds up on the page?"

"Did you have any control over what happened to you?"

She shook her head. And that loss of control was almost as frightening as being transported back to that alleyway.

"Control isn't the issue," Weston said. "What matters is the information. And I have a feeling I've only seen a portion of what's stored inside that head of his. I have to puzzle it all together and try to figure out what it's telling me and what we're supposed to do with it."

"Like gathering and evaluating evidence."

He nodded. "Only the evidence Chris gathers can't be seen or experienced by just anyone. And since I'm getting it secondhand, it's not always accurate. Sometimes it comes in scrambled or he makes a mistake. Which is what I thought this was."

"Meaning what? Coming to Santa Flora?"

He nodded again. "I already suspected the murders at the Branford house had nothing to do with the man with the tattoo, but I also knew the minute we stepped inside, that something else was off. I can't see what Chris sees, but I have my moments, and the feeling I got was that the people who died in that house were not the victims of a roving psychopath. Those killings were much more personal."

"I've been saying that all along."

"Because you have the gift, too," Weston said. "We wouldn't be talking if you didn't."

"Christopher told me the same thing. But that's absurd."

"Of course it's absurd. All of this is. But it's the reality we're dealing with. Chris is the transmitter and you and I are the receivers. Only based on what you told me, the signal you're getting is a hell of a lot stronger than mine."

"Apparently so."

"So it makes sense that he chose you. Just like he chose me."

"But for what?" she asked.

"What do you think?" Weston told her. "To help him find and kill the man with the tattoo."

So there it was, in a mere handful of words.

The idea that these two were on some kind of crusade had been percolating in the back of Kate's brain for awhile now, but it had never occurred to her that *she* might be part of that crusade.

If what she'd seen in that alleyway was true, then the three of them were forever linked by the savagery of a single man—a revelation that both rocked and rattled her. But going after that man and expecting to find and kill him, seemed hopelessly naive—and dangerous.

The fantasy of an eleven-year-old.

But then Christopher could do things no other eleven-year-old could. Like convince a grown man that chasing a psychopath was a good idea.

"You do realize that talk like that could land you right back in a jail cell."

"How?" Weston said. "We haven't done anything."

"I don't know if you've heard, but vigilantism is against the law."

"So what are we supposed to do? Sit back and let this maniac destroy more lives? If his crimes go back as far as twenty years, there's no telling how many people he's killed. He has to be stopped, lieutenant, and it's obvious the police aren't interested in doing it."

"And you think I am?"

"I wouldn't know," he said. "Coming here wasn't my idea, re-member? And I'd just as soon be gone."

She gestured to the boy. "So how do you even know him? How did you two meet?"

Weston took a moment to respond and she saw that he, too, was struggling to find his center. She expected him to start stonewalling again, but he didn't. Instead he looked around the diner as if to make sure no one was eavesdropping, then spoke in as even a tone as he could muster. "After Anna and the girls were murdered, I was in a pretty bad way."

"I can imagine you would be."

"It wasn't just the police who were convinced I'd killed them. I got stares everywhere I went. People I'd considered friends who looked at me as if I were some kind of monster."

"Even after they let you go?"

He nodded. "I owned a saw mill, and most of my employees quit. Didn't matter that Danbury was still trying to recover from the recession, they'd rather be jobless than be associated with a devil like me. So I thought, screw 'em. I stopped going to church, stopped praying altogether, shut down the mill, and shifted into self-destruct mode. I spent most nights getting drunk in my living room—the room where Anna's body was found—watching TV, shouting at the religious shows, cursing them all for being such superficial hypocrites."

"So what changed?" Kate asked. "What snapped you out of it?"

"I saw Christopher. On TV."

"TV?"

"He was on a regional cable show out of Tallahassee called Second Chances, which is about a half-step above a revival tent show. The host was an Elmer Gantry wannabe who trotted out three people he labeled as miracles of God's grace, the third of which was Christopher." He paused. "They had saved him for last, I guess, because his story was the most compelling."

"And what was it? His story."

"Abandoned at birth. Spent the first seven years of his life living in a group home for children with special needs. Then one night someone wiped them all out. Kids, caretakers, nine people in all. Christopher was found curled up in a corner, barely alive, but by the grace of God—or so the host said—he had managed to survive."

"Jesus," Kate murmured.

"The people telling the story were Chris's foster parents. Couple of unemployable reprobates who take in kids like stray pets because the government pays them by the head. I could see that they were only in it for the money—especially with Christopher, who seemed to spook them both whenever they looked at him, like he was more a curse than a miracle. But, hey, they were on TV."

"So you felt sorry for him."

Weston forced a hollow laugh. "I was too busy feeling sorry for myself. No, what happened was I got about half a bottle into my nightly quota and started hearing a voice inside my head. I thought I was hallucinating, and knew it had to be the booze, but I couldn't take my eyes off the TV. And every time they cut to a shot of Chris sitting there next to those worthless wretches, I felt like he was looking straight at me. Calling to me. Only I couldn't quite understand the words."

Kate thought about the scrambled transmission. The backwards speech. Was that what Weston had heard, too?

"So what did you do?" she asked.

"What I always did. Passed out. But when I woke up the next morning, I found an empty can of black spray paint at the foot of the sofa. No idea how it got there. But that didn't much matter when I saw what I'd done with it."

"Let me guess. A picture?"

He nodded. "The entire wall above the sofa was covered with a painting. Black and white. Detailed beyond belief. And if I'd still been a religious man, I would've said it was a sign from God, because even stone-cold sober I never would've been able to paint something like that."

"What was it?" she asked.

"A beat-up plantation style house with a mailbox out front. The name below it read HANEY, the name of the foster parents. Angela and Rupert Haney."

"So what did you do?"

"Got drunk again. And the next day, I got some paint thinner out of the garage and went to work with a rag and a sponge until all that was left of the picture was a vague black smudge."

"But it obviously didn't end there."

"No," he said. "Two days later, I woke up and there was another empty spray paint can on the floor and the painting was back. Only this time it was dark green and even more detailed than before." He paused. "But that wasn't the worst of it. In this new painting, the front door of the house was hanging open and sitting in the foyer, looking out at the street with those blank eyes, was Christopher. Staring straight at me. And I knew that if God wasn't sending me a message, that goddamn kid *had* to be."

Kate felt a chill, but said nothing.

"So I packed my backpack, locked up my house, then climbed in the Rambler and headed for Tallahassee."

"Just like that?"

"Just like that. I didn't feel I had a choice."

He reached for the glass of water next to his untouched sandwich and took a sip. He seemed far away, as if he were replaying the moment in his mind.

"And what happened when you got there?" Kate asked.

"I didn't have any trouble finding the place. It was like I had a GPS in my head and just followed my instincts. Next thing I knew I was parked out front, looking at that same house, in living color this time, mailbox and all. The only difference was that the front door was closed."

"And Christopher?"

"I got out and opened the gate and went up the steps and was about to knock when a neighbor spotted me and told me I was wasting my time. That the Haneys had piled all their little circus freaks into their car—his words, not mine—and moved across town the previous day."

"So did you go look for them?"

Weston shook his head. "I was heading back to the Rambler when something made me turn and look at the house again. And for some reason I felt as if I couldn't leave. So I went up the steps and checked the front door and found it unlocked. When I pushed it open, I saw Christopher in the foyer, sitting in the middle of the floor on that little suitcase of his. Waiting for me. Just like in the painting."

"They'd left him behind."

Weston nodded. "And they're probably still collecting a check in his name. I just stood there, staring at him, then gathered him up, helped him into the Rambler and we've been traveling together ever since. That was a little less than a year ago."

"Did he communicate with you? Say anything?"

"In his usual way, yes. And this time it was crystal clear."

"What did he say?"

Weston glanced at Christopher then looked again at Kate. "Six words. Six words that will probably stay with me for the rest of my life."

"Which were?"

"'I know who killed your family.'"

28

KATE'S CELL PHONE RANG, BUT she ignored it.

On the third ring, Weston said, "Aren't you gonna answer that?"

She pulled the phone from her back pocket, checked the screen, then jabbed the decline button and set the phone on the table. "It can wait. Keep going."

Weston spread his hands. "There isn't much else to say. It took me awhile to get my mind around what Christopher wanted me to help him do, but once I did, I was—"

"Back up a minute. You just said he knew who killed your family."

"Right. But he couldn't give me a name. And as you saw in the drawings, there are only glimpses of what the guy looks like—based on what he's gathered from the crimes scenes we've visited. Chris calls him the Beast."

"Like in Lord of the Flies?"

"Or maybe the Book of Revelation—although despite that train wreck of a TV show, I've never gotten the impression he's religious."

"But it's curious the name he's chosen starts with a B. Has he ever mentioned someone called Michael Bonner?"

"No," Weston said. "Who's that?"

She stared at him, wondering how, in less than an hour, she'd gone from complete distrust to wanting to share everything with him. But who else could she talk to about this? Certainly not her father. Or her colleagues.

So she explained what she'd seen in her vision, describing the nameplate on Bonner's chest and his attempt to cut out her mother's tongue. She even told him of her near meltdown and her conversation with Rusty Patterson.

"Right before I came to get you," she said, "I went down to the Open Unsolved file room and dug up my mother's murder book. I hadn't looked at it in years."

"That's understandable."

"I checked the witness sheets and found that Michael "Mickey" Bonner had been working security for less than three weeks when he supposedly found her in the alley. His statements during both interviews were consistent and hadn't raised any red flags. He claimed he was on his usual rounds when he spotted the body between the Dumpsters, and after checking to see if the victim was still alive, he told his partner to call the police."

"And what did the partner say?"

"He backed up Bonner's story, and probably believed it."

"Maybe I need to talk to this guy," Weston said. "If he's had direct contact with the Beast..."

"Good luck with that. A newspaper clipping in the binder said he died in a car accident two months later."

Weston looked disappointed. "And what about Bonner? What happened to him?"

"After his second interview, the investigators didn't have any contact with him, and there's nothing in the file to indicate where he might be. So I ran a database search and hit a dead end. None of the Mickey Bonners I found have ever lived or worked in Santa Flora, let alone the Sandy Point Mall."

"And no photographs?"

She shook her head. "Nothing. It's like he never existed."

"Then I guess that means it's time for us to go."

Kate frowned. "Really? After what I just told you?"

"The trail you're on is twenty years cold, lieutenant, and the only person who may have been any use to us is long dead. So what's the point of sticking around? There's nothing for us here."

"Yet here you are."

"Not for long." Weston took another sip of his water and got to his feet. "You said we could leave if I let you buy us lunch. Well, lunch is over and we need to hit the road."

"Sit down, Mr. Weston."

"I told you that coming here wasn't my idea. This is a detour. *You're* a detour. A distraction we didn't need."

"A distraction *you* don't need. But what about Christopher? He didn't show me that alley for no reason. He wants something from me. And I want to know what it is."

"You *know* what he wants. The same thing he wanted from me."

"To help you find and execute a man? That's not what I do."

"Exactly. So why not just let us go? We've been doing fine without you. And even if you *are* some kind of industrial powered receiver, I've got no problem with—"

Her phone rang again, cutting him off. Kate glanced at the screen and saw that it was Curt Clark, the same caller as before. She knew this had to be about Chucho Soriano, and couldn't put it off again.

As she reached for the phone, she looked up at Weston and nodded toward the diners at a nearby table. All wearing uniforms. "You try to go anywhere, I'll have one of these unis slap cuffs on you."

Weston stared at her, then sat back down as she put the phone to her ear and answered it.

"Messenger."

"Hey, Kate, it's Curt. Which do you want first, the good news or the bad?"

"I want you to tell me you found Soriano."

"Oh, we found him all right. His brother moved into a condo on the west side and it took us forever to locate it, but we're here now, and so are Emilio and Chucho."

"Excellent," she said. "So what's the problem?"

"That's the bad news part. They're both dead."

29

EMILIO SORIANO'S CONDO WAS ONE of a cluster of five Cape Cod style townhouses surrounding a small, gated courtyard. The place didn't scream millions, but it was considerably more upscale than any of the buildings you'd find near the Greyhound station—Emilio's former stomping grounds.

Somebody had moved up in the world.

One of the dozen or so flies that had gathered at the scene waved Kate into the parking lot and pointed her toward a spot near the medical examiner's van. She had wasted some time trying to figure out what to do with Weston and Christopher, and had finally decided to bring them along. She'd thought about throwing Weston back in a cell, but hadn't felt right about leaving the boy at the station house or sending him to CPS.

The back seat of her SUV probably wasn't much better, but it would have to do for now, assuming she could trust Weston not to get itchy feet.

After she pulled to a stop and killed the engine, she turned and looked at them—Weston quietly stewing while Christopher continued to block out the world. He held his photo album in his lap, and she wondered with a shiver if he had any more pictures for her to see.

"You think you can stay put?" she asked Weston. "Or do I have to cuff you?"

Weston wasn't close to being a happy camper, but seemed resigned to his fate. "I don't usually make the same mistake twice."

"I thought you might see it that way. We'll be resuming our conversation once I'm done here."

"This is turning into a pretty long lunch."

"Don't worry, I'll keep my word. But it'll take awhile. We still have a lot to talk about." She gestured. "And maybe Chris will have rejoined us by the time I'm back."

"So we're just supposed to sit here?"

"Beats the alternative, doesn't it?"

Kate normally left her keys in the vehicle at a crime scene, but decided to take them with her, just in case. After a glance at the boy (back and forth, back and forth), she got out and approached the officer who had waved her into the parking lot.

"You see those two in the back seat of my car?"

"Yes, ma'am."

"They don't go anywhere."

"You got it, lieutenant."

·

When she stepped through the gate into the courtyard, several members of the forensics team were moving in and out of the townhouse, doing what they did so well. Curt Clark was waiting for her on the front porch with a pair of paper booties and plastic gloves. He was a serious young man who always handled his job with a grim efficiency—which was why she'd wanted him on her team.

Kate took the booties, bent forward and started pulling them over her shoes. "Details?"

"IDs confirm it's Chucho and Emilio. Gunshot wounds to the head and chest. Nine mil. Looks like Emilio got it when he was answering the door. Chucho was in the bedroom closet."

She looked up at him. "Hiding?"

He nodded. "That's what we're thinking. While Emilio went to the door. The M.E. says the wounds are fresh, so it didn't happen too long before we got here." He paused. "There's something I didn't mention on the phone."

She finished with the booties and stood upright. "Which is?"

"We heard about what happened during the eleven o'clock, and you've got my support, no question, but I don't think you'll be happy to hear this considering how you and—"

"Get to the point, Curt. I've got an investigation to run."

"Right," he said. "Maybe it's better if you see for yourself."

He stepped aside and gestured. She looked past him through the doorway and saw Bob MacLean standing near a row of barstools, talking to one of the forensics techs.

Her chest tightened. "What the hell is *he* doing here?"

"Believe it or not, he's the one who found the bodies."

"*What?*"

"That was my reaction. He was coming out of the apartment just as we pulled into the parking lot. He flagged us down and told us to start prepping a crime scene. Said he came here to talk to Chucho and found them both dead."

"How the hell does he know Chucho?"

"He didn't explain. Just told me and Donahue to lay some tape and canvass the neighbors, see what they saw and heard."

"And what did they see and hear?"

"Not a damn thing. Two of the units are vacant and the rest of the residents are at work. Nobody home."

Kate thought about what Dan had said this morning, that she was a reactor. And the reaction she was having right now was far from good. She struggled to contain the rage that was building inside her as she pushed past Clark without another word.

Heads swiveled in her direction as she snapped on the gloves and stepped through the doorway. Emilio Soriano lay face up on the gray carpet, a tiny round bullet hole in the middle of his forehead, blood pooling beneath him. Kate knew by the expressions on the techs' faces that they were expecting her to explode. Word had already gotten around about the incident in the break room.

She forced herself to remain calm and made eye contact with MacLean. "Everyone out. Now. Except you, Bob."

The room cleared quickly as she stepped around Emilio's body and approached MacLean.

He held his hands up. "Now, look, Kate, before you go off half-cocked, just let me explain."

"How do you know Chucho Soriano?"

"I was gonna tell you this morning after you sprang that phone on me, but you got under my skin and I overreacted and—"

"You had ample opportunity to tell me. *How you do know Chucho Soriano?*"

MacLean took a breath. "He's my CI. Or at least he used to be."

"Since when have you been running a CI, and why don't I know about it?"

"There's nothing to know. If you'd done your due diligence and checked his records you would've seen I was the arresting officer on his first bust, back when I was a uni. We developed an understanding and I started using him for intel on the Varrio Disciples during the Descanso Avenue turf war."

"That was years ago."

MacLean nodded. "Exactly. But he'd been useful, so I kept up the relationship, strictly off the books—although our contact the last couple years has been minimal."

"Not according to his rap sheet. He was busted for coke less than six months ago and walked away without a scratch."

"That wasn't me," MacLean said. "Maybe someone else is running him."

"Yet you knew how to find him and didn't say anything. Why is that, Bob?"

"Look, I know I screwed up with that phone in Bree's bedroom, and I gotta tell you, I was pretty surprised when you said you found Chucho's name and number on it. So after our blow-up, I tried calling him, figuring if *I* was the one to pull him in, it might work in my favor, keep me at East Division. But he didn't answer, so I went looking for him." He gestured to Emilio's body. "Looks like somebody else found him first."

"Did they?"

MacLean frowned. "What's that supposed to mean?"

Kate held out a hand. "Give me your weapon, Bob."

"You think *I* did this?"

"I try not to jump to conclusions. But if you don't want me to work my way toward what I'm hoping is the wrong one, you'll give me your weapon."

"You just crossed the line, lady. Hell, you're *way* over it now."

"Ask me if I care."

MacLean eyed her, then reached to his hip and pulled his Glock free, handing it to her, grip first. Kate lifted it to her nose, didn't notice any telltale smells of gunpowder, then released the magazine and racked and locked the slide.

There was a round in the chamber and the mag was full. If MacLean had anything to do with these shootings, he hadn't used this gun. She replaced the magazine, racked the slide forward, but held onto the weapon.

MacLean's frown deepened. "You're not gonna give that back?"

She ignored the question. "Is Jake around? Has he shown up yet?"

"I'm right here, Kate."

She turned with a start and saw Jake Linkenfeld lurking in the hallway, a pair of gloves on his hands.

"Way to scare the crap out of me. Have you been there all this time?"

He shrugged. "I could hear you from the bedroom, but I didn't want to interrupt your conversation."

"I assume you heard the pertinent part?"

He walked over to them. "Come on, Kate, Bob may be a pain in the ass sometimes, but he isn't good for this."

MacLean glanced at him sideways. "Thanks, buddy."

"Believe it or not," Kate said, "I'm inclined to agree. But right now I want you to go outside and organize a search of the surrounding area."

"What are we looking for?"

"What else? The weapon. In case it was ditched."

"By Bob?"

"By anyone."

"Well then you might want to add something to the list."

"Meaning what?"

Linkenfeld gestured. "Check this out."

They followed him down the hall to a bedroom where Chucho Soriano's body lay halfway out of the closet in a pool of blood. There was a small desk nearby with a keyboard, mouse and monitor, but no computer.

"The tower's missing," Linkenfeld said. "Bob would have to be a helluva Houdini to make both it and the weapon disappear."

Kate turned to MacLean. "Give him your car keys."

MacLean hardened. "You gotta be fucking kidding me."

"You want this over with? Give him your keys so he can check your car and eliminate you as a suspect."

"This is a goddamn vendetta," he said. "Why would I kill these guys?"

"Why would anyone kill them?"

"I'm thinking drugs," Linkenfeld said. "If Chucho was connected to the Varrio Disciples, could be he and Emilio were in deep with one of the cartels."

MacLean shook his head. "He cut his ties with the gang. That's why he wasn't as useful as he used to be. Last I heard from him, he and his brother had gone into the Internet porn business. Running a site called the Latin Prowlers."

Kate's brows went up. "What's that about?"

"He and Emilio would dress up like gangbangers and cruise the streets of West Santa Flora in a lowrider, looking for girls to fuck. Only these girls were porn models and it was all prearranged to look spontaneous. Chucho would bang 'em in the back seat while Emilio ran the camera."

Lovely, Kate thought. "What do you bet that missing computer is their server? The one that hosts the website."

"Could be," Linkenfeld said. "But why take it? It's no threat to anyone. The porn business is legal."

"Unless they were using underage girls, like Bree Branford. That might explain the phone calls."

They all thought about this and MacLean shook his head. "The Branford girl was squeaky clean."

"Come on, Bob, you know as well as I do that what her friends and family saw could've been completely different from what she showed the Soriano brothers. And that cell phone is proof." She looked around. "How many bedrooms does this place have?"

"Three."

"A three-bedroom townhouse in this part of the city doesn't come cheap. Even the monthly HOA would bankrupt most people. And it's my understanding it's pretty tough to make any decent money in porn these days unless you're a very big player. I can't imagine these two could make the mortgage on this place without some serious income."

"So what are you thinking?" Linkenfeld asked.

"That whatever was on that computer was enough to kill for, and maybe they were using the information to target someone. Collect a little extra cash. Maybe the killer's name or IP address or even photograph is on there. Somebody who stood to lose quite a bit if it ever became public."

"So they were blackmailing him?"

"With Chucho as point man, or maybe even the sole player. Emilio could've been in the dark. But then the victim turned on Chucho and that's why he was hiding in the closet when the doorbell rang."

If she was right, Kate wondered how deep Bree's involvement was. Could she have been part of the blackmail scheme?

Was that the reason for the massacre?

"That's a helluva theory," Linkenfeld said.

"And a plausible one, don't you think?"

MacLean snorted. "What I think is that you need to stop making assumptions and start looking at the evidence. Then we can come up with a theory."

Kate smiled. "That's a good idea, Bob. Now give Jake your keys."

30

MACLEAN'S CAR WAS CLEAN AND a search of the area yielded nothing.

Kate had expected as much, but had to be sure, and despite her dislike of the man, she was relieved. The last thing she needed was to find a killer under her command.

Not that this cleared MacLean completely, but it was a good indication that he was a wrong turn. Still, she didn't want him anywhere near this investigation.

They were standing in the courtyard now, looking out toward the parking lot, when she gave him his weapon back and told him to go home. His presence was no longer needed.

"I found the goddamn bodies," he said.

"And we have your statement, Bob. If we need anything more, I'll be sure to call you."

"I belong here and you know it. This isn't right."

"Neither is withholding information. But that's what you did, isn't it? Every time you make a move or open your mouth you just prove that I made the right decision this morning."

He narrowed his eyes at her. "I am so gonna enjoy watching you belly flop."

"I'm sure it'll be quite a view from the cheap seats. Drop me a line when you get there."

There wasn't anything to add to this, so Kate turned and walked away, putting some distance between them as she pulled out her phone, dialed Computer Forensics and asked to speak to Matt Nava.

She felt MacLean glaring at her and turned to look at him just as he gave up and walked away, heading toward the courtyard gate.

After a series of clicks, Nava came on the line.

"Hey, Matt, I need a favor. I want you to do a search for a website called the Latin Prowlers."

He seemed a bit winded. "Sounds dubious," he said. "Hang on."

"Are you okay?"

"Yeah, I'm just coming back from a late lunch and decided to take the stairs instead of waiting on the elevator. Last time I'll ever do that." She heard the clatter of a keyboard. "Okay, here it is. Let me click the link." She waited and he said, "Looks like the server's down. I'm getting a 404 not found."

"I got the same thing on my phone. Is there any way we can find out what was on there?"

"Not unless there's an archive or a mirror site."

"What's a mirror site?"

"Exactly what it sounds like. A clone that visitors are redirected to in case the main server goes down. But if they had one in place, I doubt we'd be getting the 404. What *is* this thing, anyway?"

"A porn website. And the guys who own it are dead."

"Oh? Does this have something to do with our friend Soriano?"

"Yeah, he's one of the dead guys. He and his brother."

"Yikes," Matt said.

"No kidding. And when it comes down to it, you're the reason we're here. If you hadn't cracked the password on Bree's phone..."

"Hey, don't sell yourself short. You're the one who found it, remember?" He paused. "I'm thinking since we're talking porn, there's a pretty good chance there's an unauthorized mirror out there somewhere."

"You mean like somebody made a copy and put it on their own server?"

"It's been known to happen. Some hacker clones the site and has access to all the data. Including credit cards, if he's in a larcenous mood."

"Is there any chance you'd be able to find this mirror if it exists?"

"No guarantee. But I can try."

"That's all I ask. I need to know what's..."

Kate paused as she felt a small tremor in her head, as if someone had just run a finger across her left temple. She looked up, letting her gaze drift past the gate toward the parking lot and her SUV. A rear passenger door hung open and Christopher stood in front of the car, his sightless eyes staring in her direction.

Where the hell was that uni she'd told to keep and eye on them?

"Kate?" Matt said.

"Sorry, Matt, I've gotta go. Call me if you have any luck."

She abruptly clicked off and took a step toward the gate, wondering what Christopher was up to.

Then, for the first time since she'd fled her office, his voice filled her head, the transmission clean and clear and full of youthful conviction.

I can feel it, Kate. I feel it all around me.

The man who did this is someone you know.

31

"SOMEONE I KNOW?" KATE SAID. "Are you sure?"

They were in her SUV now, with the doors closed, Christopher on the seat next to her. He had returned from the haze looking more animated than she'd ever seen him.

Yes, he said. *I'm sure.*

"But I thought you had to be closer to the actual crime scene to do this gathering thing?"

This is part of it. The man was waiting out here in the parking lot, hiding near the trash cans until it was safe to go inside.

Kate stared out and saw the doorless trash bunker near a group of trees that bordered the parking lot. They had searched it for the computer and the murder weapon and come up empty, but it was an easy enough place to stay out of sight until you were ready to make your move.

Anyone standing there would have a direct view of the courtyard and the Soriano apartment.

"Okay," she said, "then who is he? What does he look like?"

Christopher shook his head. *I don't know. The pictures aren't clear.*

"Can't you make them clearer?"

Weston, who had been sitting quietly on the back seat, leaned forward. "It doesn't work like that. Like I told you at lunch, this is all hit and miss. Whatever network he's connected to doesn't always broadcast at full bandwidth. Like a wireless signal cutting in and out."

Kate again thought of the radio transmission. The garbled words. This was all so new and foreign to her that she felt dazed and disoriented. Not a place she liked to be. She thought she must be suffering a kind of shell shock from her ridealong in that alley, and when in doubt, her natural inclination was to play the skeptic.

She looked at Christopher. "So if it isn't clear, what makes you think it's someone I know?"

Because I felt him when I was at your office.

"What do you mean *felt* him?"

His energy. All around me. And he's been there before. Lots of times.

Kate thought of Bob MacLean and wondered if she had dismissed him too quickly. Had she given him exactly what he wanted—a way out?

She tried to think of who else Christopher might have been exposed to, but the East Division wasn't small, and neither was its employee pool. She looked at the unis and forensic techs working in and around the townhouse and still wasn't fully convinced.

"What about here?" she asked. "Is he here now?"

Christopher hesitated. *I don't know.*

"How can you be sure it's someone from my office? There are a lot of people from the department here. How do you know you aren't just confused?"

Because I feel his sickness.

"His sickness?"

The pain he carries. The guilt and the fear. He tries to hide what he is, but he can't hide what's inside him. And only people like us can see it.

Kate thought the kid was giving her far too much credit. She couldn't see or feel a thing without the help of his magic photo album. She glanced at it lying on the back seat next to Weston and felt a small shiver run through her. She wasn't anxious to go through something like *that* again.

"Is that all you can tell me? Are you sure there isn't more?"

No. The pictures aren't strong enough.

Weston gestured toward the townhouse. "He might be able to if you take him inside, let him gather more evidence."

She shook her head. "There are two dead bodies in there."

"Are you forgetting he's blind?"

"Just because he can't see doesn't mean he can't be traumatized."

"Oh, please, lieutenant, did you even listen to what I told you at lunch? He's been through far worse than either of us can imagine and it looks to me like he's holding up just fine."

"He's a child, for godsakes. None of this is good for him."

"Neither is getting your tongue cut out and being left for dead. Yet it seems to me he's handling this stuff a lot better than—"

"Look, even if I agreed, what am I supposed to tell my team? The minute I drag a kid in there they'll think I've lost my mind. And trust me, that isn't much of a stretch."

"Hey, if you don't want his help that's fine with me. I'd just as soon be on the road and—"

Stop, Christopher said sharply. *Stop fighting.*

They both went quiet, and Kate felt like a bickering parent chastised by a battle-weary child. And judging by the look she saw in her rearview mirror, Weston felt it, too.

It was hard to tell, but Christopher seemed to be caught in a memory—and not a good one. Maybe his foster parents, the Haneys, had been fighters. Or worse.

The ring of her phone cut through the silence. She let it ring a few times, then pulled it out and answered without looking at the screen. "Messenger."

"Hi, Kate, it's me, Matt."

"Hey, Matt, can I call you back? I'm kinda in the middle of something."

"You'll want to hear this. I found the mirror of the Latin Prowler website."

"Already? That was fast."

"What can I say—I'm good at what I do. I'm not sure why the hacker didn't do a reroute to avoid the 404, but maybe he's still in the middle of setting it up, or maybe he just did it to see if he could. Either way, you'll never believe what else I found. Something that could blow this case wide open."

"Meaning what?"

"The Branfords weren't the all-American family everyone thought they were. In fact, they were anything but."

"Now you've got my attention."

"Good," he said. "Because you need to get back here right away."

•

"Where are you taking us now?" Weston asked.

"To your motel. I called ahead to make sure a room is available —and don't worry, I'm paying for it."

They were driving up the 101, headed toward the Pacifica Avenue exit, Christopher again sitting next to Weston on the back seat.

"I don't care who's paying for it. I told you, we need to leave."

"Yeah, you're a broken record, but I'm pretty sure Chris feels differently, and I can't be dragging you all over Santa Flora with me." She looked in her rearview mirror. "Am I right, Chris? Do you want to stay?"

Yes.

She looked at Weston. "See?"

He sighed. "I don't get you. One minute you're interrogating him about your crime scene, the next you're pushing him in a corner until it's convenient for you to deal with him. What do you want from us?"

"If I knew, maybe I wouldn't be so goddamn conflicted."

"Then get some therapy. If you want Chris's help, shuttling us off to a motel won't do you any good. And if you *don't* want it, then why are we even here?"

"Because I need to know more," she said. "About what he can do and about what happened to my mother."

"You already know what happened. You *saw* what happened."

"And with every minute that goes by, it seems less and less real. I honestly don't know *what* to think anymore."

She took the offramp, drove half a block to the Circle Eight and pulled into a spot near the front office.

Weston scanned the lot. "Where's our car?"

"It was impounded last night. I called to have it released and someone will deliver it in the next couple hours. So if Chris changes his mind, I don't suppose there's much I can do to stop you from leaving."

"You know he won't."

"I'm hoping not." She reached over the seat and patted Christopher's knee. "I'll be back tonight, okay? We can talk then."

Christopher smiled, and Kate not only saw the smile but *felt* it.

A warmth that reminded her of her mother.

Don't be long, he said. I have a lot to tell you.

32

THE SANTA FLORA COMFOR lab was little more than a small, cramped room that held a series of work benches cluttered with gutted computers and a variety of hard drives, most of which had been seized during the execution of a warrant. The only thing that differentiated it from your typical Geek Squad repair room were the EVIDENCE bags the drives were stored in.

Matt Nava was one of the two men who staffed the unit and, by default, was currently the man in charge. Matt's boss, an affable guy named Connelly, had been missing in action for the last few weeks as he recovered from wrist surgery. And despite Connelly's generally pleasing demeanor, Matt didn't seem to miss him much.

When she stepped inside, Kate found Nava hunched in front of a laptop that was wirelessly connected to a big screen TV on the wall.

"Show me," she said.

He grinned. "What—not even a hello?"

"Consider this an extension of our phone conversation."

Matt nodded and worked the keyboard. "It isn't pretty—unless you're into this kind of thing. The guy who mirrored it did a good job of covering his trail, but I think I can track him down if we have to."

After a few more keystrokes, the Latin Prowlers website filled the TV screen, showing an over-saturated image of an emerald green low rider with two Hispanic gangbangers—the recently deceased Soriano brothers—posing in front of it, wearing sunglasses and large, satisfied smiles. Several photos were composited around them, showing garish close-ups of naked women of various ages and races engaged in a number of sexual activities that left nothing to the imagination. Most of this activity was taking place on the backseat of the low rider.

"Lovely," Kate said. She wasn't a prude, by any means, but she certainly wasn't the target audience for this stuff.

Matt looked a little embarrassed. "I warned you."

"Okay, so where's the link you found?"

"Right here."

Matt ran a couple of fingers along his touchpad and the image onscreen began to scroll down the page. In the right hand column were animated graphics advertising a dozen more affiliated websites. Chubby Girls, Ebony Amateurs, Asian Angels, Hardcore Lesbian Bikers, and tattooed women who smoked cigarettes and verbally abused men as they masturbated.

"I did a Whois on each of these sites," he said, "and found they're all owned and operated by the Soriano brothers through a company they founded called Latin Lovers, LLC."

Kate nodded. "Looks like they had their own little empire."

Matt stopped on an ad for a website called *XXXurbate*, a web-cam chat service that promised:

> *Live couples and solo chatters who will*
> *blow your mind as you blow your wad.*

This was getting better and better.

Matt clicked the link and the screen switched to a simple, non-flashy interface featuring several dozen rectangles in a grid on the page. Each rectangle showed tiny thumbnail images of women or couples in various stages of undress, some merely sitting in front of a computer cam while others were engaged in sexual activity of one kind or another.

"So what's this?" Kate asked.

"It's either a sad commentary on the state of mankind or sexual nirvana, depending on your point of view."

He ran the cursor over one of the thumbnails, which showed what looked like a middle-aged couple. The man was seated at the computer while the woman was stretched out on the bed behind him, completely nude, and doing something rather disgusting with a liquor bottle. A banner that read   CURRENTLY OFFLINE obscured most of the image.

"Take a closer look at these two," Matt said.

He tapped his touchpad to take them inside the chat room of "Mike-n-Maisey." The screen showed a large video window with a running chat module along the right side. The video window was blank except for the word OFFLINE.

"Here's how it works," Matt said. "The couple comes online and does an interactive sex show using the webcam on their computer while viewers make comments and requests in the chat window. They give tips using pre-purchased credits, and a percentage of each tip is paid to the performers. The more tips, the more you see, and the viewers are usually using their keyboards one-handed, if you catch my drift."

Kate caught it all right. The ad for the site had spelled it out. "So it's essentially a mutual masturbation club."

"And people like Mike-n-Maisey can make a considerable amount of extra income for doing what comes naturally. Especially if they do private shows. Some performers work out of their own homes, while others go to special office suites where the offices are set up to look like bedrooms. The performers come in, punch a clock, and put in their eight hours."

"You seem to know a lot about this."

"I'm a strong believer in research."

"Yeah," Kate said. "That must be it. So why show me Mike-n-Maisey? Why not show me somebody who's still online? I think I can handle it."

"Because Mike-n-Maisey are offline for a reason." He scrolled down the page to a profile section that featured nude photos of the couple, along with links to several of their archived videos, which could be bought for a hundred tokens each.

And now that Kate saw them clearly, she recognized them, largely due to the bedroom they were posing in—one she'd been inside a number of times in the last few days. The man wore sunglasses and the woman was sporting a cheap black wig, but it was obvious to Kate who they really were.

"Christ," she said. "Thad and Chelsea Branford."

"Sharing their unbridled passion with a thousand and one neck beards who can't get a date on Saturday night. You ask me, it's like watching your parents do it. Who wants to see that?"

"Apparently someone does."

Kate thought about all the sex toys they'd found in Chelsea Branford's nightstand and the reason for them was clear. They were props for the webcam show, broadcast from their own bedroom. The question was, why hadn't her team found any indication of this until now?

"Okay, Mr. Research, so how do these performers set something like this up?"

"Easy," he said. "You sign up on the chat site and use their broadcasting software to stream from your computer. You could even do it from a laptop with a built-in webcam and microphone. Set it on your dresser facing the bed and you're good to go."

They hadn't found anything unusual on the Branford home computer, so maybe Thad and Chelsea had used a laptop that had also gone missing. If so, it seemed the killer was amassing quite a collection of hardware.

Kate glanced around the room at all the computer parts. "So why hasn't anyone come forward about this? You'd think with all the people watching, somebody's bound to've recognized these two from the initial news coverage."

Matt shrugged. "Maybe, maybe not. You have to realize that this cam stuff gets broadcast all over the world by thousands of couples, and most of the people who watch it would never make the connection. And don't forget that anyone participating in chat porn probably isn't all that anxious to talk about it."

"Small wonder," Kate said. "There was no indication that the Branfords were even involved in this kind of thing. How hard would it be to hide?"

"Not hard at all. And considering all the wackos out there, it's a smart move. They could've used a private internet company to mask their identities and paid for the service with gift cards."

"Gift cards?"

"The kind you can pick up at a supermarket or a big box department store for cash. The gift card code gets transferred to the Internet service and you're completely anonymous. And if they wanted to keep their extracurricular activity off their tax returns, there's a dozen different ways to make that happen."

Kate sighed. "I feel like an infant when it comes to this stuff."

"Most cops are. Which is why guys like me are gainfully employed." He gestured to the screen. "But we aren't done yet. Mr. and Mrs. Branford are only the tip of this particular iceberg."

Kate waited as Matt punched a few more keys and the view on the TV screen switched to another chat room with a blank video screen marked OFFLINE.

"Meet Barely-Legal-Barbi. Who, as it turns out, isn't legal at all."

He scrolled down the page to the profile section which featured photos of a beautiful dark-haired girl posing provocatively in a Catholic schoolgirl uniform. She looked older than sixteen—but not by much.

Bree Branford.

"It gets worse," Matt said. "One of her archived videos shows her doing the dirty with Chucho on the back seat of that low rider. I didn't see any sign of it on the Latin Prowlers site, but I'm guessing they would have added it sooner or later. And I have to assume she lied about her age."

Kate's stomach went sour.

Why would Bree feel the need to do such a thing?

For money? Attention?

Or had she been coerced into it? The victim of a couple of warped parents?

Kate had seen worse in her career, so the idea wasn't that far-fetched.

But the hidden cell phone suggested that the Branfords knew nothing about Bree's involvement with Chucho, and Kate wondered how the two had met. Was it by happenstance? Had Chucho and Emilio discovered that one of their cam couples had a beautiful daughter and sought her out? Or had Bree found out what her parents were up to and decided to follow in their footsteps?

With all of the participants dead, Kate doubted she'd ever know the answer to this. But no matter how it had happened, Bree Branford was a working girl—an *underage* working girl—and the thought of that sickened Kate.

She suspected that, in the course of her work, Bree had encountered the wrong customer. A customer who was lured into an extortion trap by two people who had shared secret phone calls, and soon found himself in a compromising situation with a girl who was barely old enough to drive.

A situation that only multiple murders and a cover-up could repair.

And according to a strange little boy who could see and feel what others couldn't, that customer was *someone Kate knew...*

33

"IS THERE ANY WAY to identify the people who logged into Bree's chatroom?"

Matt chuckled. "Doubtful. These places don't usually keep permanent logs, and even if they did, we're talking thousands of chatters a week. It would be pretty tough to narrow it down to a few suspects."

"The Latin Lovers had a pretty extensive network of websites. Are these *all* clones?"

"Looks like just the Latin Prowlers site, but I'd have to dig a little deeper to be sure."

"So would that mean that the computer stolen from the Soriano apartment was only one of their servers?"

Matt nodded. "It's likely that with the amount of traffic we're talking about, each website has its own. Normally they'd all be in one location, but with these guys it's hard to say. I'm not sure why they operated the Prowlers site out of their apartment."

Kate looked at the photos of Bree posing in her schoolgirl outfit and studied the room surrounding her. Except for the bright purple bedspread and matching curtains behind the bed, the place had less character than a doctor's office.

"That's definitely not Bree's bedroom. You think she could've been working out of one of those office suites you mentioned?"

"That's what it looks like, but it's a lot harder to hide your age up close and personal, so she would've had to jump through some hoops to convince them she was legal."

"Or maybe nobody cared."

"There's that, too."

"So if this office suite is out there somewhere, what are the chances there's a server or two on the premises?"

"Pretty good, I think. But we don't necessarily need to locate them. I could look for a way in from here and see what I find."

"Forget it," Kate said. "Chasing down a cloned website is one thing, but if you do any black hatting without a warrant, we may wind up regretting it. Let's see if we can locate this office and take it from there."

She pulled out her phone and called Linkenfeld and got no answer. She dialed again, calling Curt Clark this time, and when she had him on the line, she said, "Hey, Curt, are you still at the crime scene?"

"Yeah," he said. "The coroner's guys are bagging the bodies, so it looks like they're about to wrap things up."

"Did the techs dust that trash bunker?"

"They did, but one of them was bitching that there were a billion and one prints in there, so I don't know how much good it'll do."

"Where's Linkenfeld?"

"He left shortly after you did. Said he was headed back to the crib."

"Why?" she asked.

"I'm not sure. He got a phone call and left."

Kate wondered what that was all about, but had other things on her mind.

"Okay," she said. "I'll be checking the databases on my end, but do me a favor and search the desk and file cabinet in that bedroom office for records of any property the Sorianos may have leased. If you find anything, give me a call."

"You got it."

"Thanks."

When she clicked off, Matt was fingering his touchpad.

"I just had a thought," he said.

"Which is?"

"There's no way to identify the majority of the chatters in Bree's room, but a lot of performers keep a list of high tippers, guys who get a little obsessive and aren't shy about buying and spending tokens." He pointed. "There's Bree's list."

Kate looked at the TV screen:

TOP 5 TIPPERS
Dirtydancer666 - 3,100tk
Lovetogetnasty - 2,100tk
Blowmenow - 2,000tk
Barbisloveslave - 1,400tk
Kojak - 800tk

The one calling himself Kojak was a curiosity. The name was from an old TV show that was still in reruns on cable and the Internet, about a detective whose trademark was sucking on a lollipop. Some of the local gangbangers used it as slang for any cop who crossed their path—and Kate had been one of those cops.

Hey, Kojak, I got a lollipop you can suck.

Could he be the one Christopher had told her about?

She looked at Matt. "Is there any way to track these people down?"

"We could put out an APB on frustrated husbands and socially awkward computer geeks, but that would probably keep us busy for the next couple decades."

"Haha. Now what's the real answer?"

"It's a possibility, if they used a credit card to purchase the tokens, or didn't hide their IP addresses when they logged in to the site. But again, we either go in through a back door or you have to find the server. Of course, that doesn't guarantee that any of these creeps are your guy."

"No," Kate said, "but it's a start."

•

She was on her way back to her office when she heard the familiar laughter of Rusty Patterson and Captain Ebersol, coming from the hallway near the elevators. She turned and started in that direction, but stopped as she reached the corner.

MacLean and Linkenfeld were with them and they were all looking mighty chummy.

Kate took a step back, hoping they hadn't spotted her, and watched them from behind a painter's scaffold, which had been parked in the hallway since the first days of building renovation.

She watch them interact, feeling foolish for hiding from them, but she couldn't help wondering what was going on.

Had Rusty just made an appeal to Ebersol on MacLean's behalf? And what about Linkenfeld? Kate thought she'd had his support, but it wasn't looking very solid at the moment.

Rusty was smiling at MacLean, and he may have been retired, but his opinion still carried a lot of weight around the department. He had been conciliatory during his talk with Kate in the chapel, but maybe he was starting to regret his decision to pass her the baton. Maybe her meltdown in the bathroom and her failure to get along with MacLean was a sign of weakness in Rusty's eyes.

What was worse was that MacLean had probably told them what had happened at the Soriano crime scene, and Linkenfeld had confirmed it. Kate didn't feel she had done anything wrong, but she'd learned long ago that, warranted or not, pointing the finger at a fellow detective was never a good idea. Yet that was exactly what she'd done, true to her own impulsive nature.

It was clear she had a tin ear when it came to diplomacy, so maybe she *wasn't* suited for this job. And after this roller coaster ride of a day—and the major mindfuck that had accompanied it— she wasn't so sure she was suited for life in general.

A vacation home in the Keys was sounding pretty good right now.

She watched as the four men shook hands, then MacLean and Linkenfeld got on the elevator and disappeared behind its closing doors. A moment later, Ebersol said something to Rusty, patted him on the shoulder, then headed toward his office. Rusty then turned, facing her direction, and Kate ducked back, knowing exactly where he was headed next.

Feeling more foolish than ever, she moved quickly down the hall past Computer Forensics and made her way toward the Major Crimes squad room. But before she got around the corner, Rusty's voice rang out behind her.

"Kate? Can you give me a moment?"

She stopped, feeling her shoulders slump, then turned and faced him. "I'm kinda busy, Rusty. Don't you have another trip to plan?"

He approached her. "I heard about that mess MacLean stumbled into this afternoon. He tells us it may be related to the murders in Oak Grove. He also said you humiliated him in front of his partner and half the crime scene squad."

"Ex-partner. And if he was humiliated, maybe he should've told us about his involvement with Soriano from the get-go."

Rusty smiled and Kate knew he was about to do what Rusty Patterson did so well. Try to smooth the waters.

"Here's the thing you have to understand," he said. "Nobody really likes change. Not the people it affects adversely, and not even those who stand to benefit from it. Anything that stirs up the status quo tends to create all kinds of fears and anxieties and people start acting out in ways they normally wouldn't."

"So is that what I'm doing? Acting out?"

"Both you and MacLean have some adjusting to do. You're used to me serving as a buffer between you, and now that I'm gone, your world is turned upside down and neither one of you knows quite how to behave. Bob tries to assert some power and you think the only way to deal with that is to prove you're just as mule-headed as he is."

"Is that what you think of me?"

Rusty sighed. "Come on, Kate, don't give me that kind of nonsense. You're better than that. And MacLean isn't—which is why I gave you the nod. So it's up to you to be the adult here and make it right. That's part of the job."

She considered this and nodded. "Maybe I *have* been coming on a little strong."

"A little?"

She gave him a wan smile. "I'm not like you, Rusty. I can't do things the way you do."

"Nobody's asking you to. But you need to ease up and choose your battles carefully. Half of this job is politics and at this rate you're gonna render yourself unelectable."

She knew he wasn't wrong, but she wasn't sure she had the kind of self-control he was advocating.

"For what it's worth," Rusty went on, "MacLean admitted he hasn't made things easy for you, and Linkenfeld gave you his unqualified endorsement. That poor son of a bitch is caught between a rock and a hard place, and just wants to see everyone get along."

"Believe it or not, so do I."

"I believe it. And I don't figure this case you're working is making things any easier for you. You having any luck with it?"

She considered telling him what Christopher had said, but didn't think throwing around even more accusations about the people she worked with would be a smart career move. Besides, she wasn't yet sure that Chris was right, and trying to explain to Rusty what the boy was capable of would be problematic, to say the least.

"Making the connection between the Branford girl and the Sorianos has thrown this case wide open," she said. "Turns out she and her parents were working for them as online sex performers."

Rusty's brows went up. "The daughter, too?"

"I saw it with my own eyes."

"But Linkenfeld told us she's jailbait."

Kate nodded. "And I think that's the reason they're all dead."

"How so?"

"I don't know what else Linkenfeld told you, but I think our perp had a sexual relationship with her and this whole mess boils down to retaliation for a blackmail scheme. There have to be some incriminating photos or a video stored on a drive or a memory stick and buried in a hole somewhere, and he's doing his best to make sure it never comes to light."

"That's pretty extreme," Rusty said.

"Is it? We live in a world where people get their heads cut off in the name of God, so extreme is a matter of opinion."

"I suppose you're right about that."

"You know I am. This guy's just your run-of-the-mill sociopath who's willing to do whatever it takes to protect his own status quo." She thought about this and smiled. "Maybe he doesn't like change."

34

KATE RAN A DATABASE SEARCH that failed to bring up any hits on the Soriano brothers' real estate holdings. She was thinking it was a lost cause, when Curt Clark called her from the crime scene with some good news.

"These guys were about as organized as a schizophrenic two-year old, but I found a lease agreement buried at the bottom of one of the desk drawers. A suite of fifteen offices in the Walker building downtown."

"Are their names on it?"

"No, it's signed by a Winifred Stratton of Stratton Employment Services."

"Probably a cover company, to get past any occupancy restrictions. I doubt the owners of the building would be thrilled to know what goes on there."

"What *does* go on there? What's this all about, anyway?"

"I'll fill you in later, but let's just say they're making money the old-fashioned way with a twenty-first century twist. What's the address?"

Curt gave it to her and when they hung up, she immediately called Linkenfeld. He answered after several rings and she thought she detected some hesitation in his voice.

The sounds in the background explained why.

"So where are you?" she asked. "Across the street?"

"Yeah, I never got lunch, so I figured I'd grab an early dinner."

"Well, get it to go. I need you to meet me at the Walker building in thirty."

"Why? What's up?"

"I'll explain when you get there," she said. "Oh, and bring Bob with you, too."

He hesitated. "Bob?"

"Come on, Jake, I know he's with you. Just tell him that if he doesn't bust my balls, I won't bust his."

More hesitation. "Are you sure? Because I gotta be honest with you, I don't like being stuck in the middle of this shit."

"I'm sure," she said, then hung up.

•

The Walker building was located in Santa Flora's garment district, which was currently undergoing gentrification. It was one of the oldest buildings in the city, a forty story highrise that had been built during a time when the idea of Internet chat sex was relegated to sci-fi smut novels.

After she briefed Linkenfeld and MacLean, Kate rode with them up to the fourteenth floor, the mood in the elevator tense but tolerable. She had taken Rusty's advice to heart and suspected MacLean had gotten the same speech.

"So what's the game plan?" Linkenfeld asked.

"Depends on what we find. If this place is what I think it is, we need to talk to any of the girls who may have known Bree. If she was hooking on the side, maybe one of them will be able to ID some of her regular customers. There was probably some sharing going on."

"Variety is the spice of life," MacLean said.

The elevator came to a stop and the doors opened to reveal a colorless reception room with a desk at the center and a couple of sofas shoved up against a wall. A sign behind the desk read CAM EQUIPMENT: YOU BREAK IT, YOU BUY IT, and to the left and right were hallways dotted with office doors, most of which were closed. The lights were all on, so somebody must have been home.

Kate exchanged glances with Linkenfeld and MacLean.

"Looks like this is the place," she said, then called out, "Hello?"

She was answered by the muffled sound of a toilet flush.

A moment later a doorway at the end of the left hall swung open and a dark-haired girl of about nineteen emerged wearing a flimsy flower print robe and nothing else. The robe hung open, revealing a cleanly waxed body adorned by a multitude of colorful tattoos.

The girl saw them, stiffened, and pulled the robe closed. "Can I help you?"

Kate showed her a badge. "Santa Flora Police Department. We're looking for a Winifred Stratton."

"Who?"

"Winifred Stratton. She signed the lease on this place."

It took some thought, then the girl said,"Oh, right, Freddie. She's the manager here. But you'll have to come back tomorrow. She's gone for the day."

"What's *your* name?" Linkenfeld asked.

The girl hesitated.

"Don't worry, we're not here to bust anyone. We just want to know who we're talking to."

"My chat handle is Dark Angel."

"I'll bet it is," MacLean said.

Kate shot him a glance and tried with all her might to remember that she had to be the adult here.

He got the message and she said to the girl, "How about a real name? Or at least something besides your chat handle."

She hesitated again. "Melissa."

"All right, Melissa. How many girls are working tonight?"

Melissa glanced at the hallway doors. "We aren't doing anything illegal."

"Why don't you let us decide that?" MacLean said. "How many?"

"...Ten, I think. Some of the girls have left already."

"Then what do you say you help us out and round 'em up so we can all have a nice big powwow?"

"Are you kidding?" she said. "Some of them are doing shows and they'll kill me if I interrupt."

"We'll make sure that doesn't happen," Kate told her.

•

It took a good fifteen minutes to get all the girls out into the reception area—a mix of races and body types, most of them in their late teens or early twenties. Some took root on the sofas while others chose to stand, none of them happy that they'd been pulled away from their work. Some wore robes, but several were topless and didn't seem to care that a couple of male detectives were openly gaping at them.

Kate supposed it came with the territory, but was tempted to ask them to cover up before MacLean and Linkenfeld started offering them tokens.

When they were settled, she said, "I know you all have a living to make, and I'm sorry to interrupt you, but we're investigating a crime and want to ask you some questions."

"What kind of crime?"

This came from a girl with spiky black hair and a bustier that looked like something out of a forties glamour magazine.

Kate looked at her and said, "That isn't something we can talk about. But it's our understanding that one of the girls who worked here went by the nickname Barely Legal Barbi. Did any of you know her?"

A topless blonde snorted derisively. "Which one? We've probably had about fifteen Barbies in the last few months."

Kate reached into her back pocket and pulled out a letter size envelope. Inside were two identical photographs—image captures of Bree Branford from the *XXXurbate* website. "Like I said, this one calls herself *Barely Legal* Barbie."

She handed one photo to the blonde and the other to one of the girls who was standing nearby, then told them to take a close look and pass the photos around.

They did so, grudgingly, and Kate knew that both MacLean and Linkenfeld would be watching the girls' faces (assuming they could stop staring at their breasts) for any sign of a reaction.

After a moment, Kate said, "Well? Anyone?"

A redhead on the sofa raised her hand as if she were in a classroom. "Isn't this the girl from the TV? The one who was killed with her family?"

"We can't discuss the case," Kate said. "Do you know her?"

"Just from the news, if this is her."

Kate looked at the other girls. "What about the rest of you?"

They responded with head shakes and nos, then passed back the photos as one of them, a lazy-eyed brunette in lacy red lingerie said, "You have to understand that a lot of girls come and go around here. We see different faces all the time. Some stay for awhile, but most get bored with it and decide they'd rather do something else."

Like blackmail? Kate thought.

"So *none* of you recognize her?"

The redhead started to raise her hand again, but Kate waved her off.

"I know, just from TV."

They were all silent and Kate turned to Linkenfeld and MacLean.

"Well?"

"The blonde with the rack," MacLean said. "And the Asian chick."

Kate nodded. "That's my call, too. Jake?"

Linkenfeld shrugged. "You guys must be better at this than I am. I didn't get a thing."

Kate told the girls they could go back to work, except for the two that she and MacLean had singled out.

The two girls groaned when Kate held them back and the Asian girl said, "What's the deal? Why can't *we* go, too?"

MacLean grinned at her. "Because you suck at poker."

35

HER CHAT NAME WAS AsiaX, but her driver's license said she was Natalie Chen.

Kate had insisted on seeing it the moment they stepped into the girl's faux bedroom, because she didn't look much older than Bree. But the license was authentic and said she was twenty-two years old, and Kate knew that Asian girls often looked much younger than their actual age.

She was dressed in only a sheer black bra and panties, and Kate told her to put something on. The girl grabbed a gingham print babydoll dress from a bed littered with vibrators and dildos and slipped into it.

Kate thought about Linkenfeld and MacLean—who had stayed in the reception area to question the blonde—and had a feeling that neither of them had asked *her* to cover up.

She gestured to the camera mounted on a tripod near the foot of Natalie's bed. "Is that thing live?"

Natalie eyed her sullenly. "Yes."

"Take it offline."

"Why? What're you gonna do?"

"Ask you some questions. Now turn it off."

Natalie scowled, crossed to a laptop on the dresser and hit a key. A red light on the camera switched off. "Happy now?"

"Yes. Thank you."

"I don't know why you have to be such a bitch. I didn't do anything."

"Except lie?"

"About what?"

"Come on, Natalie, I saw your face when you looked at that picture. And it wasn't because you saw her on TV like your red-headed friend. She worked here and you knew her."

Natalie said nothing.

"Look, if you're afraid of someone and you'd rather do this somewhere else, that's fine with me. We can talk downtown if you want to."

"Downtown?"

"At the police station."

"Why do I have to go *there*? I didn't *do* anything."

"Yeah, you said that. But if you withhold information, that's what's known as obstruction of justice and it can land you in jail. Is that what you want?"

She looked alarmed. "No."

"Then lose the attitude and tell me what you know about the girl in the photograph. Because you know something."

"All I know is I'm losing a lot of money right now."

"The sooner you say something useful, the sooner I'll leave and you can go back to work."

Natalie studied Kate, weighing her options, then made a gesture with her fingers. "Let me see that picture again."

Kate knew it was a stalling tactic, but she pulled out one of the photographs and handed it to her.

Natalie made a show of studying it. "You know, when I look at this now, I think you may be right. I do remember her. She was a regular here for awhile."

"Imagine that," Kate said.

"But she only did weekends. I think she went to school during the week."

"So you knew she was underage?"

The eyes widened. "I didn't say that."

"You haven't said a whole lot, but I have a feeling you knew her better than you're letting on. You two were friends, weren't you?"

"We talked to each other sometimes, but—"

"But nothing," Kate said. "You're no better at hiding it now than you were five minutes ago. Something's going on inside that head of yours, and I want to know what it is."

Kate waited for a response and was surprised when the hardness in Natalie's eyes abruptly disappeared and they began to fill with tears.

"Oh, God…" she said. "Oh, God…"

Kate waited.

"I warned her like a hundred times. I told her he was a creep."

"So you and Barbi *were* friends."

Natalie wiped at her eyes, her lower lip trembling. "Not like BFFs or anything, but we used to talk a lot and we did a couple of group shows together and I swear to God I didn't know how young she was until a lot later. She didn't *act* like a kid…"

"Who's the *he* you warned her about?"

"Chucho Soriano."

"What about him?"

"He's the creep who owns this place. He and his brother. He used to hang around a lot when Barbi was here and I told her he was trouble and that she should just do her job and stay away from him, but she thought he was cute and wouldn't listen to me. And he's the reason she's dead. I know he is."

The news of Soriano's murder hadn't reached the airwaves yet, and Natalie was operating on the notion that he was still alive.

"What makes you think that?" Kate asked.

"Because he's crazy, that's why. He told her he loved her, but he made her do all kinds of terrible things."

"Like what?"

"He started pimping her out to her chat buddies even though he knew she was underage, and they were planning something bad. She used to brag about how they were gonna get rich and live in a big house and I figured it was just talk, but then they started messing with the wrong guy and I knew something terrible would happen."

"What guy? Who were they messing with?"

"One of her regulars. She used to do a lot of one-on-one cam chats with him, then Chucho arranged for them to meet and… and…" She started to cry again. "I knew I should've told someone, especially when I found out how old she was, but I was afraid Chucho would try to hurt me, and—"

"What was his name, Natalie? The man he wanted her to meet?"

She sniffed and wiped her wrist across her nose. "I don't know. She only told me his chat name."

"Which is?"

"I'm not sure. Kogo or Kojo or—"

"Kojak?"

"Yeah. I think that was it. I remember she put him on her high tipper list and the guy got mad and wanted her to take it off."

"Have you met this man?"

She shook her head. "No. I've never even seen him. All I know is what Barbi told me."

"Not even a picture or a video?"

"*No*," Natalie said.

"Then I don't get it. How did you know he was the wrong guy to be messing with?"

Natalie hesitated, looking as if she'd just made a very bad bet and wanted to take it back.

"Natalie?"

"Why should I trust you? Look who you came here with."

"What do you mean?"

"That guy in the reception room, interviewing Crystal."

"Which one? The big guy?"

She shook her head. "No, the other one."

Linkenfeld. She was talking about Linkenfeld.

"What about him?"

The girl got quiet again and Kate softened.

"Look, Natalie, you're not in trouble, okay? And you won't be, if you tell me the truth. Just say what you want to say."

Natalie considered this, then nodded. "It's just he comes off all smooth and stuff, but he's a complete creep. I've got a friend who works a corner a couple blocks over and he threatened to arrest her if she didn't give him a blow job."

"And you know this how?"

"She pointed him out to me one night. He's always harassing her and her friends."

Kate felt something shift inside her. Could this be true? Linkenfeld had always struck her as one of the good guys.

"Are you saying you think he might be the one Bree shouldn't have been messing with? That he might be Kojak?"

"No. I don't know. Maybe. All I know is what Bree told me."

"Which was what?"

"That the guy they had on the hook was a cop," Natalie said.

"She told me he's a fucking cop."

•

A cop.

Chat name Kojak.

Confirmation that Christopher's "feeling" had been dead on.

Confirmation Kate didn't *want.*

Especially if that cop was Jake Linkenfeld.

Because, until now, she'd been able to pretend that Christopher had somehow gotten it wrong. That it was one of his misses. A scrambled transmission. A guess that had grown out of the confusion of his surroundings.

Kate wasn't forgetting that she herself had put Bob MacLean on the suspect list, but she'd never truly believed it.

And now that Linkenfeld's name had been floated, she couldn't believe that either. Even if he was doing what Natalie's friend had accused him of—as disgusting as it was—that didn't make him a murderer.

Did it?

Whatever the case, Kate had been forced to confront the idea that he or MacLean or one of a few dozen other policemen— someone she knew, someone in the very building she inhabited for a good part of the day—could well be the killer she sought.

So what was she supposed to do now?

•

After questioning Natalie for several more minutes and failing to get anything new out of her, Kate let her dry her tears and switch her camera back on, then went outside to the reception area, where Linkenfeld and MacLean were waiting.

She couldn't help looking at them both in a different light.

"Any luck?" Linkenfeld asked.

Confirmation or not, Kate was no more inclined to share Natalie's accusation than she had been when Christopher had made it. Especially if one of these men was her suspect.

She shook her head. "What about you guys?"

"Blonde's name is Crystal Hatcher," MacLean said, "And either she's a pathological liar or we both read her wrong. She swears up and down she never saw or met the Branford kid, and we pushed her pretty friggin' hard."

"Okay, so maybe we'll get lucky with the data on the website server. It has to be here somewhere," Kate looked around. "What happened to the girl with the tattoos? Dark Angel?"

"I think she had a date with a demon vibrator," MacLean said. "But don't sweat it. Crystal showed us a closet in the employee break room that she says houses the main computer. Problem is, it's locked tight and the manager, Freddie, is the only one with the key. I tried calling her, but got no answer."

"And apparently she's a real stickler about warrants," Linkenfeld added.

Kate sighed. "This time of day, I was hoping we'd be able to finesse that part. So it's a waiting game at this point."

MacLean spread his hands. "Isn't it always?"

"I'll tell you what," Linkenfeld said. "I know a guy who's clerking for Judge Takane, and I can probably twist his arm into expediting a search and seizure. We can be back here by tomorrow morning when Ms. Freddie walks in the door."

Kate considered this and wondered if Linkenfeld's willingness to go the extra mile was a sign of his lack of culpability.

Then again, maybe he knew there was nothing incriminating on that server.

This situation was screwed up in more ways than she could count, but without any concrete evidence, what could she do but wait to see how it all shook out?

"I guess that'll have to do," she said. "I just wish it were tonight."

MacLean snorted. "And I wish my new friend Crystal would park that cute little butt of hers on my bed." He headed toward the elevators. "But like they say in France, wishes don't fill the bag."

36

IT WAS DARK BY THE time Kate reached the Circle Eight motel.

As she pulled into the lot she noted with some concern that there was no sign of the Rambler and wondered if it hadn't yet been delivered from the impound garage, or if Weston had decided to ignore the boy's wishes and take off anyway.

She went to the room she'd left them in—number 148 this time—and didn't see any lights in the window.

Shit.

She tried knocking on the door anyway, not expecting an answer, but was surprised when Christopher's melodic voice filled her head.

I'm here, Kate.

Then the door opened and Christopher stood in the darkness, no sign of Weston anywhere.

Kate stepped inside and flipped on the light. "He *left* you?"

Just for a little while. They brought our car and he went to get us some food.

"I can't believe he left you alone."

Why shouldn't he? Because I'm blind?

"I just don't think it's a good idea."

I'm not a baby, Kate. The Haneys used to leave me all the time.

"Based on what I've heard about them, that doesn't make me feel any better." She closed the door and dropped her bag on the dresser. "He shouldn't have left you alone, and when he gets back he's gonna hear about it."

Chris crossed to a chair in the corner and sat.

You need to be nicer to Noah. He takes good care of me. And I don't like it when you guys fight all the time.

She again felt like a chastised parent, and thought about her conversations with Dan and Rusty. "If people just did what I want them to, there wouldn't be a problem."

Nobody does what we want them to.

She laughed and sat on one of the beds, a little unsettled that she'd accepted this unorthodox form of communication with Chris so easily. Less than a day ago, the idea of telepathy—for lack of a better word—had been a joke to her.

"I guess that's true," she said.

But I'm glad Noah left me here, because I knew you'd be coming soon and I wanted us to be alone.

"How did you know I was coming?"

I felt it. Just like I feel the change in you.

"Change?"

You didn't want to believe me before about the man who killed those people. Even though you know what I can do, you were starting to doubt it, and you were hoping I was wrong.

"Can you blame me?"

No, but that's changed, hasn't it? You believe me now.

"And wish I didn't," Kate said. "Life would be a lot less complicated that way." She looked at him. "But why do you want us to be alone?"

Because I didn't tell you everything.

"About what?"

I told you before I was born this way. But that isn't true. What I was born with was more like what you and Noah have. A strong sense of intuition.

"Okay," Kate said. "So then how did you get like this?"

"It happened the night I died."

•

Kate felt a draft of cold air and had no idea where it was coming from.

She shivered involuntarily. "Died?"

Yes.

"What the hell are you saying?"

I know Noah told you about what happened to me and all of my friends. At the home we lived in.

"Yes, but he didn't go into much detail."

Because he didn't know that many. And what he didn't know until tonight is that the man with the tattoo didn't just leave me for dead. I was dead. He strangled me and threw me down and when he was sure I was gone, that I had no heartbeat, he cut out my tongue.

Images of Christopher being thrown to the floor filled Kate's mind and she closed her eyes and tried, without success, to will them away. She couldn't be sure if they were products of her imagination or were coming from the boy himself.

While the Beast was busy cutting me, I went to a place that was dark, and warm, and safe... And there was someone waiting for me.

Kate opened her eyes. "Who?"

A stranger. A woman I didn't know, but who said that we were bound together by this man's violence. Connected by our shared experience. I couldn't see her, not even in death, but I felt her. And I heard her voice.

"Who was she?"

Someone you love, Kate, and who loves you with all her heart. She told me her name was Cassie.

Kate's throat went dry.

Cassie was a name she knew all too well. What everyone had called the beautiful young cop's wife, the police dispatcher who had been taken from them far too early.

Cassandra Messenger.

Kate's mother.

•

The room around Kate began to sway.

No. No. This was too much. Too much for any human being to absorb in a single day. She gripped the edge of the bed, hoping she wouldn't teeter to the floor.

"I don't believe you," she said.

I knew you'd resist, Kate, but it's true. I can feel her in you. And she's in me, too. She's who I look for when I go into the haze. And she helps me see the pictures when I'm gathering. That's why the signal is so much stronger when I send them to you.

"No," Kate said, and she couldn't stop shivering.

When I died that night, Cassie told me it wasn't my time. That I had to go back because the Beast wasn't done killing. That he would never be done unless someone stopped him. She said my blindness would help me see without filters, and that others would help me understand what I saw. People who knew the pain he caused...

"No..." Kate said.

She stayed with me and held me and told me about her little girl. And about the boy who was still with her.

"...What?"

She was carrying your brother inside her the night she was killed. Your baby brother. I could feel his heartbeat as she held me.

Kate got to her feet. "Stop. Stop right now."

You need to hear this, Kate. You need to know what he took from you. All of it.

"STOP!" she shouted. "Please stop!"

He's a beast. That's what she called him. The Beast. And when I woke up in the hospital and realized I was still alive, I knew that she was right. That he had to be found. That he couldn't be allowed to go on, doing what he'd done to her and her baby and to me... And to you.

Kate said nothing, her mind reeling, her heart thumping.

She was done asking how any of this was possible. She was done talking at all. The thought that her mother—her *pregnant* mother—was the catalyst behind all this had crippled her, rendering her speechless.

I've been trying to find you ever since that day, Kate. To find Cassie's little girl. But she's never told me how. She's never even told me your full name. She helps me see things, but it's like she wants me to find my own way, too.

Kate was stunned. Still unable to speak.

Then a few nights ago when Noah left me in our room in Reno, I heard a news report about the Branford murders. And even though I knew those murders had nothing to do with the Beast, I heard a policewoman on TV asking for viewers to come forward with information.

And I recognized her voice. It felt and sounded just like Cassie's voice.

But I knew that wasn't possible, so I told Noah to bring me to Santa Flora, and I could feel that alley calling to me. And the moment we went there I knew that my instincts had been right. That that alley was where the Beast had killed Cassie. And that the voice on TV wasn't hers—wasn't Cassie's—but her daughter's.

I had found Cassie's daughter.

And that's why I'm here, Kate. That's why I'm here.

They heard a beeping sound and the door opened and Weston came into the room with a key card in one hand and a bag full of take-out boxes in the other.

He stopped when he saw them, took one look at Kate's face and said, "The British have a name for that expression. They call it gobsmacked."

37

"I WAS ALL SET TO leave the moment they brought the Rambler," Weston said.

They sat across from each other on opposite beds, Christopher in the bathroom with the door closed.

Kate's mind was still reeling, but her heartbeat had slowed to a manageable pace. She felt distracted, not quite in the room, thinking about her mother's pregnancy—her brother on the way—and wondering why her father had never mentioned it. Wondering why it wasn't mentioned in the autopsy report.

"I didn't care what Chris wanted," Weston said. "There's too much drama here and I wanted to put you and this town in our rear view mirror."

Kate blinked at him. "So what stopped you?"

"Chris told me what he just told you. About what happened the night he died. He's never shared that with me before."

"I almost wish he hadn't shared it with me."

Weston shook his head. "Don't talk like that. You aren't some random victim in all of this. You're part of it. That's clear to me now. You were destined to be."

"Don't be so sure."

"I didn't say I like it. You're rude and you're stubborn and you jump to conclusions like every other cop I've encountered. But I understand why he came looking for you."

A toilet flushed and a few seconds later the bathroom door opened and Christopher came out wiping his hands on his pants. He looked small for his age, and defenseless, but he was proof that what you see is not always what you get.

He fixed his eyes on Kate. *I want to help you.*

She still felt off-balance. "...With what?"

I want to help you find the man who killed those people.

Kate hadn't given the Branfords and the Sorianos a single thought since she got here. That part of her world had been relegated to her work brain, the section that understood and processed all that was mundane, like sex and blackmail and cops nicknamed Kojak who went off the deep end and committed multiple homicides.

"I told you, I don't want to expose you to that."

And I told you I'm not a baby.

"No, but you're eleven years old."

(Although at the moment he seemed like the old man in the room.)

That doesn't matter. Let me help you find him, Kate. I know I can do it. We can do it together. Take me back to the place where those two men were killed.

She shook her head. "Even if I agreed, there are people who live in the other apartments and the media is probably knocking on their doors as we speak, so there'll be cameras all over that place. And if someone sees me take a kid into that apartment—"

Then take me to the house instead. The Branford house.

Kate paused, remembering the first moment she saw him through the window, standing in their living room. Less than twenty-four hours had passed since that moment, yet she felt at least a decade older.

I was already there once. What will it hurt to go again?

"He's got a point," Weston said. "You interrupted him before he could do much in the way of gathering, so another try might give you exactly what you need to find this guy. Especially if you can process the images the way you did today."

Kate shivered. "I'm not sure I want to go through that again."

"It isn't a matter of what you want. Do you think I wanted to be painting pictures on my living room wall?"

"You're saying I don't have a choice?"

"There's always a choice. But the wrong ones tend to come back and bite us in the ass. And you know what Chris is asking is the right thing to do. This nonsense about traumatizing him is just an excuse."

"For what?"

"To keep from going to a place in your mind that scares you. Because that's the bottom line, here. You're afraid of all of this. Believe me, I know exactly how you feel."

Christopher approached her now, then reached out and found her hands.

Let me help you, Kate. Let me help you catch him. There's more than one kind of beast out there, and we should always do what we can to stop them.

"Who are you?" she asked. "Where do you come from?"

He smiled and squeezed her hands.

The only thing that matters is where we're going.

38

THEY TOOK THE RAMBLER, WESTON looking pleased as he slid behind the wheel, as if he'd been reunited with an old friend.

They said very little on the drive into Oak Grove, as Kate tried to put the night's revelations into some kind of perspective, knowing the task was futile. What was happening to her could not be analyzed or catalogued or weighed with any real logic. She was in an emotional and intellectual free fall now, where anything was possible.

They took the 33 into the valley past Amelia's Oak, then made the turn onto Cartham Road, which wound through the woods thick with oak trees. There were only a few houses in here, the Branford home the most isolated of them all.

Kate wondered what had compelled Thad and Chelsea Branford to transform themselves into Mike-n-Maisey, and decided to chalk it up to a case of simple economics. She had no idea what kind of money a custom cabinet maker pulled in, but all of the businesses in the area had been hit hard by the recession. And during the slow, laborious recovery that followed, the extra income may have been crucial to their survival.

Bree's involvement, on the other hand, was still a cypher. Her "good girl" act was clearly just that, but Kate had to believe that, like any sixteen-year-old, she could be easily manipulated by the right guy.

Not that any of it mattered at this point. They had all gone into the darkness and the man who had sent them there was still walking free.

A man that Kate might know.

And Christopher was right. The killer may not have been the beast that he and Weston were after, but he was, without a doubt, a beast.

One who needed to be put away.

As Weston nudged the wheel through the twists and turns in the road, Kate looked out at the trees lit up by the moon, and wondered how much they had seen that night. Or worse yet, how much pain and suffering and violence had they witnessed over the course of their ancient lives?

She braced herself as they took the final turn toward the Branford house, wondering what she was getting herself into, wondering if she'd be able to handle the visions any better than she had this morning—and not all that anxious to find out.

Then a voice in her mind said, *It's okay, Kit Kat. You'll be fine.*

But it wasn't Christopher she heard.

It was her own voice, filtered through her memories of her mother.

•

They were less than a block from the Branford house when she saw it.

"Pull over," she said suddenly. "Kill the headlights."

Weston did as she asked, the brakes squeaking faintly as they came to a stop at the side of the road. She reached for her bag and pulled out the Steiner binoculars she always carried with her.

She put them to her eyes and pointed them at the Branford house, looking for the light she thought she'd seen coming from that direction. She saw only darkness at first, then there it was again, the faint beam of a flashlight, bobbing and weaving for a moment before it disappeared.

Someone was inside the house.

"What's going on?" Weston asked.

"We have an intruder," Kate said, then turned to Christopher, who sat on the back seat. "Did you know about this? Is that why you wanted to come here?"

I wasn't sure. But yes.

"A word of warning would have been nice. Is it the man we're looking for?"

I think so.

Kate felt her pulse quicken. Weston had characterized the boy's accuracy as hit and miss, and she had no idea what his track record was like, no data to rely on, but her own intuition—her own experience with him—told her he was right about this.

And whoever was in there was undoubtedly hoping to find something else that she and her team had missed. Something incriminating.

A homemade porn video?

A compromising selfie with an underage girl?

Kate considered her options, the stupid cop/dead cop mantra once again tumbling through her mind. She knew she should call for backup. Get Linkenfeld and MacLean out here, or maybe Clark and Donahue or even their requisite weirdo of a night man, Billy Zimbert, who would just be coming on duty.

But what if it was one of *them* inside that house?

If this guy was someone she knew, a phone call to the wrong person would warn him that she was out here, and that wouldn't be good.

She lifted the binoculars again and studied the area. No cars in the driveway. None on the street. Whoever it was had probably parked on one of the other access roads and taken a hike through the woods to reach the house.

Kate put the binoculars back in her bag and touched the grip of the Glock holstered at her side. The magazine was full and she always kept a round in the chamber.

Not that she wanted it to come to that.

"I need you two to listen carefully," she said. "You do *not* get out of this car. Okay?"

Weston's brows went up. "You're going in there alone?"

"We can debate the pros and cons when this is over, but believe it or not, I have a bit of experience on my side."

Then again, if the intruder was a cop, so did he.

She turned to Christopher. "Do you have anything more to tell me? Any feelings you want to share?"

He shook his head.

"Be sure now, because you're not all that forthcoming some-times. You might want to work on that."

Just be careful.

She nodded and opened her door and the interior lamp came on, lighting them up. She quickly got out and closed it again, hoping the intruder wasn't watching, but they were nearly a block away, and chances were good he was too busy concentrating on his search.

She took a moment to assess her situation, then started to move.

She didn't want to take the direct approach, so she stepped sideways, into the woods, dodging broken branches as she worked her way toward the house. There was just enough moon tonight to make the journey possible, but she stumbled a couple of times and was tempted to unclip her mini-mag for the extra light.

Resisting the temptation, she forced herself to slow down. She was nearly to the house when she stopped and studied it, seeing nothing but darkness inside, and wondering if she'd taken too long.

Was the intruder gone?

Had he found what he was looking for and headed back into the woods?

She heard a faint crackling sound behind her and stiffened.

She heard it again—like boots trampling twigs—and pulled her Glock free as she spun around and saw a silhouette looming in the darkness.

"Don't move," she said, then unclipped her mini-mag and turned it on, shining it into the face of Noah Weston.

Shit.

She quickly doused the light, heart pounding, and kept her voice low. "What the hell is wrong with you? You were supposed to stay in the car."

"You think this is my idea? Chris was worried about you, and when he worries, I pay attention."

"And in the meantime, if our guy's still inside and he saw that light, we may have scared him away."

"I think we're okay," Weston said. "Take a look."

She turned and peered through the trees at the front bay window. The flashlight beam was back, bobbing and weaving, as the intruder crossed through the living room. She saw a dark shape, but couldn't quite define it.

She holstered her Glock and gestured to Weston. "Stay here. If you move from that spot, I swear to God I'll shoot you."

"Maybe Chris is worried about the wrong person."

"Maybe he is," she said, then continued through the trees toward the house.

•

She had nearly reached the place when she decided to go wide and circle around to the back, where the woods would give her better cover. There was no longer any sign of the flashlight beam, but she felt confident that someone was still inside.

If he had left, she was close enough to the house now that she would have heard noises of some kind. A door opening and closing. Footsteps on the wooden deck that surrounded the place.

Yet the absence of light and the silence that accompanied it were unnerving.

Did he know she was out here?

Every step *she* took brought with it the crackling of tree branches and leaves—just as it had for Weston—and she doubted her approach was as quiet as she had hoped it would be.

Maybe doing this alone was a mistake, but what other choice did she have?

She kept reminding herself that calling in the cavalry when the guy inside might be *part* of that cavalry was not a workable strategy. Although a part of her, despite Natalie's confirmation, still wanted to believe that Christopher was wrong about the killer.

None of the cops she knew, from Captain Ebersol on down, seemed capable of doing what this man had done. Even Bob MacLean, for all his annoyances, had never struck her as a psychopathic pedophile. It was too much of a stretch.

But then she thought of Bree Branford and her friends' insistence that she was good girl. And Thad and Chelsea, who had led a secret life as Mike-n-Maisey, unknown to the people around them.

And that was the truth of the matter, wasn't it?

We never really know what lurks beneath the skin of the people we work with. Or the people we live with, for that matter.

She thought of Dan, and his betrayal after six years of marriage. The pain she felt when she realized he'd spent two of those years—two whole years—lying to her. Deceiving her. Taking someone else into their very own bed. And he was a psychiatrist, for God's sake.

A professional. A man of insight and integrity.

A man she had loved and who had claimed to love her.

If her own husband could hide something like that, what about the detectives on her squad? What about Linkenfeld, who had reportedly taken to harassing prostitutes in his spare time? Or the patrol officers who walked in and out of their building every day? Or the crime scene techs, or even members of their support staff, from Drew Kelp in Services and Communications to Matt Nava in Computer Forensics?

And what about the man who had murdered her mother? Mickey Bonner? He had presented himself as a witness all those years ago, a simple security guard who had stumbled into something horrific, and his story had never been doubted. Yet beneath that uniform was an evil so deep that it could almost be classified as supernatural. Not of this world. And for a brief moment, as she had occupied his body, Kate had felt that evil.

She remembered what Rusty had told her up in the chapel about his now dead partner. That this job and the things they saw in the course of it were like a virus that ate some cops alive.

Could it also turn you into someone else? Send you spiraling into a darkness so addictive that you did things you never thought you'd do, and would go to any length to keep from being discovered? And how much effort did it take to hide it all? How many of the smiles you smiled masked the disease you carried? The blackness of your heart?

Maybe she'd have an answer when she took this son of a bitch down.

Maybe.

Crouching in the trees at the back of the house now, she studied it carefully, shifting her gaze from window to window, hoping to see that flashlight beam.

But there was nothing. Only darkness.

She knew he was in there somewhere. She could feel him, as Christopher had, her newfound sixth sense kicking into overdrive. After calculating the time it would take her to cross to the back door, she emerged from the trees and moved at a crouch as quickly and stealthily as possible. Leaves crunched beneath her shoes, and she winced at the sound, keeping her right hand on the grip of her Glock.

She reached the deck, took the steps up to it and sidled up to the wall between a window and the back door. Wondering if it was safe to take a peek inside, she decided it was worth the risk and ducked her head toward the window, looking into what she knew was Bree Branford's bedroom.

The intruder was nowhere in sight, but there was enough moonlight filtering in to reveal the chaos he had left behind. The shelves had all been cleared, the closet and the dresser drawers hung open, the contents of the room scattered haphazardly across the wooden floor. Clothing. Lipstick and bottles of make-up. Stuffed animals with their guts torn out. Picture frames. Posters of rock bands and movie stars that had been ripped from the walls. Bree's mattress and bed overturned, and the rug beneath it tossed aside.

There was a desperation to it all that led Kate to believe that the killer was reaching a fever pitch. Maybe he hadn't found what he was looking for on the Sorianos' computer, or maybe he believed that Bree had hidden a duplicate of whatever it was, just as she'd hidden the phone. Whether he'd found it in her bedroom was anyone's guess, but Kate didn't think he'd still *be* here if he had—assuming that sixth sense of hers was right.

So where was he now?

She knew the back door was locked—or at least it *had* been last night when she'd conducted her own search. Fortunately, she'd made a duplicate key and had been carrying it since the first day of the investigation.

She crouched in front of the door and checked the knob.

Definitely locked.

Which meant the intruder had likely gone in through a window.

Taking her keys from her pocket, she found the one she needed, carefully slid it into the lock...

(Not a sound, she told herself. Don't make a single sound.)

...then turned the knob and started to push, but felt resistance. Then she remembered that Thad Branford had, for reasons known only to him, designed it to be an outswinging door, and had secured it by welding the hinge pins to the hinges themselves.

Unfortunately, she remembered this a moment too late.

Just as she was about to open it, the door flew wide, knocking her backwards. Kate grunted in surprise as a dark figure barreled into her at a run and slammed her to the deck. The back of her skull hit it hard, sending a bright burst of pain through her head.

The intruder jumped up and over her and scrambled down the steps as Kate cursed under her breath and rocketed to her feet, trying to shake away the pain as she leapt off the deck and followed.

He was already disappearing into the darkness of the trees, and she tried to determine from his size who he might be, but her head was pounding and her vision had begun to double, making it impossible to determine much of anything.

She lit out after him, each footstep jarring her brain, and then she, too, was in the trees, dodging fallen branches as she barreled into the darkness, hoping she was even headed in the right direction.

Then she saw him as he moved into a wan pool of moonlight, still nothing more than a dark figure, impossible to identify.

Yanking her Glock from its holster, she shouted "Stop, goddamn it! Stop!"

But she knew she was wasting her breath, there was no way this guy was going to slow down. And as he disappeared into the darkness again, she saw the flash of a muzzle and dove to the ground.

A bullet whizzed past her and took a chunk out of a nearby tree.

Keeping a tight grip on the Glock, she scrambled for cover and returned fire—once, twice—and thought she may have hit him but couldn't be sure. She waited for what seemed an interminable amount of time, hoping she'd gotten lucky, but those hopes were dashed when she heard the distant sound of a car starting.

Kate exhaled a string of curses, knowing he had reached the access road, and she had blown her one chance to bring him down—whoever the hell he was.

She heard the sound of footsteps behind her and spun around to find Weston again, holding his hands up, palms facing her.

She really needed to break him of this habit.

"I heard shots," he said, a little out of breath. "Are you hurt?"

Her head was still pounding, but she knew it would pass.

"Only my pride," she told him. "Only my pride."

39

IT WAS WESTON WHO SUGGESTED they do what they had originally come here for.

He and Kate had gone back to the house to assess the damage the intruder had caused, and discovered that every room in the place had been thoroughly trashed. If there had been anything here for the killer to find, he had likely found it.

They were standing in a fresh new crime scene now, and Kate knew she'd have to call this in to the CS techs and put them to work looking for fingerprints and DNA. She'd also have to report what had happened to her team, and to Captain Ebersol—but she didn't have to tell them *why* she'd come here, or that she hadn't come alone.

"You should probably take Christopher back to the motel," she said. "Once I make this call, they won't waste any time getting here."

"Why make it at all?"

"Gee, I don't know. Because it's my job?"

"And how will you explain how *you* got here? I drove, remember?"

She hadn't thought about that. "I'm not sure, but I'll figure something out."

"Or you could put it off for a while, and once we're done here we can take you to your car and you can drive back out by yourself."

"Once we're done?"

"Doing what we came here to do."

Kate thought about this. "I'm not sure I want to go there anymore."

Weston sighed. "I don't think you were ever sure."

"And what if I wasn't?"

"You have to stop running away from it, lieutenant. Christopher has a gift and so do you. You may have lost your killer out there, but don't forget he's still in here. All around us. And if we're lucky, and Chris is firing on all cylinders, we may find out who he is."

"I don't think you know what you're asking of me."

"I know exactly what I'm asking."

"But you don't know *me*. I'm not sure I can go through that again."

"Was it really that hard?"

Kate bristled. "I saw and felt a man try to cut out my mother's tongue. What do you think?"

"Then let me do it," he said. "Find me some paper and something to sketch with and let us loose in here. We've done it enough times before."

She considered this and nodded. "All right, but let's make it quick."

•

Kate waited as Weston retrieved the Rambler, parked it in the drive, and helped Chris up the steps and into the house. The boy was carrying his pink photo album and she eyed it dubiously.

"You couldn't have left your book in the car?"

I like to have it with me. Are you all right?

"I will be when this is done."

Stop being afraid, Kate. There's nothing to be afraid of.

"I shouldn't be afraid of sushi, either, but one bout of food poisoning and I've sworn it off forever."

She was trying to make light of the situation, but felt weak and foolish and knew he was right. But she would've been lying if she said she wasn't glad that Weston had volunteered to serve as Chris's conduit. If his experience was even half as emotionally wrenching as hers had been, she didn't envy him for a moment.

Besides, her head hurt and she was still smarting over the loss of her suspect.

The electricity had definitely been turned off and there was no light in the house. Kate found some candles in the kitchen and placed them strategically around the living room, lighting them as she went. The furniture had been ripped to shreds, so Weston dragged a couple chairs in from the dining room.

Kate was too amped to stay still, but forced herself to sit anyway as Chris moved to the center of the room, lit only by the moon and flickering candlelight. Weston sat next to Kate, pulling a legal pad and pen into his lap. They had found them on the floor in Thad Branford's office.

"Are you ready?" he asked Chris.

The boy nodded and closed his eyes for several seconds, then opened them again to stare up at the ceiling. All at once he seemed to go away somewhere, into the haze, and she remembered him standing just like this the first time she saw him.

Had she known then what she knew now, she may have turned and walked away.

He began to rock slightly, back and forth, back and forth, and the temperature in the room seemed to shift, dropping half a degree or so. Kate wasn't sure if she was imagining this or it was an actual physical manifestation of the emotional energy being drawn from the room. She thought of how people often speak of their feelings in terms of heat and cold and wondered if there was some truth to it.

"How long does this take?" she asked Weston.

"Depends on how strong the energy is, and how far back he goes. If he limits it to what happened tonight, it could go pretty fast."

"Are you saying he might try to draw from the night of the murders?"

"That makes the most sense, doesn't it? Then there's no mistake who the killer is."

Kate was about to respond, when Christopher made a guttural noise, deep in his throat. Except for the voices in her head, she had never heard him utter a sound and it threw her off balance. She remembered that Dan had said he was capable of vocalizing but seemed to choose not to.

She glanced at Weston and he looked alarmed as well. Then Chris made another sound, as if he may be in distress.

Kate jumped to her feet. "Is he okay? Has he done this before?"

"No," Weston said, "but I'm sure it's fine. Give him time."

Chris uttered another sound, this one long and low and coming from deep inside him. Then suddenly he took his gaze from the ceiling and swiveled his head toward Kate, his mouth starting to move as if he were attempting to form words. But no words came forth, only guttural noises that approximated speech.

"Ahahahahaaa."

Under the best of circumstances he would have been difficult to understand, but here, the sound was both horrifying and heart-breaking and sent a chill straight through Kate's central nervous system. Even Weston was on his feet now, and had clearly never experienced anything like this.

"What do we do?" she asked.

"What *can* we do? We have to go with it."

"But what is he trying to say?"

The words came again, no clearer than before, Christopher's blank eyes fixed on Kate.

"Ahahahahaaaahahaaa."

She moved slightly, and the eyes followed her, and she suddenly realized that he could *see.*

And then it hit her. The person looking at her, the person trying to speak, wasn't Christopher at all.

It was someone else, trying to communicate *through* him.

He took a step forward and extended an arm, holding the photo book out toward Kate, as if asking for her to take it.

She started to back away but Weston grabbed her arm and said, "Do it, Kate. You need to do what he wants."

She wrenched free. "Are you out of your fucking mind?"

"I'm not sure what's going on, but if you want to catch your killer, this may be the only way."

The boy took another step forward, pushing the photo album toward her. Kate hesitated, wanting to flee, to be anywhere but here, and hating herself for it. But could anyone really blame her? This was fucking insanity.

Weston wouldn't let up. "Do it, Kate. You know you have to do it."

And he was right. She knew he was right.

Christopher—or whoever this was—uttered more noises and Kate finally stepped forward, hesitated again, then reached out and took the photo album in her hands.

The moment her fingers gripped it, she felt heat rise up through her arms and into her chest, then radiate throughout her body. As it reached her brain, the throbbing in her skull abruptly disappeared and the room began to sway and rotate around her, spinning faster... and faster... as her vision narrowed and lost focus.

Then everything went dark and she felt herself falling as the darkness swirled around her. And somewhere far away, a man's voice drifted toward her...

"...build you a fucking castle..."

"...build you a fucking castle, baby..."

"...build you a fucking—"

And then she opened her eyes and found herself lying on a bed in the soft glow of a nightstand lamp, a phone to her ear, the voice on the line saying, "Before we're done with this guy, I'm gonna build you a fucking castle, baby."

"But what if he stops paying?"

This question had come from Kate, but it wasn't her voice. This was Bree Branford's bedroom, so it had to be Bree. And that meant only one thing:

Kate was in the middle of another ridealong.

She was *inside* Bree's body.

"He'll never stop paying," the voice on the line said. "That culero thinks he's a big shot, and he don't want no teenage panocha to tarnish his reputation and land him up in Coalinga. So what other choice does he have?"

"He's a cop, Chucho. He could come after us."

Chucho snorted. "I been dealing with cops half my life, and most of them don't got two fingers of a forehead, but this one ain't stupid, and I get the feeling that what he did with you is only some of the shit he's into. I made it clear to him that there's more than one copy of those videos and if he tries anything—"

"You didn't tell him *I* have one, did you?"

"Relax, baby. All he knows is you're some cute little piece of panocha he likes to get nasty with. He don't even know your real name."

"Yeah? Well Natalie says he could find out."

Chucho exhaled. "I told you to quit listening to that little bitch. She's getting you all riled up over nothing."

"Are you sure I'm safe?"

"As long as you got that data chip, you'll be fine. Where'd you hide it, anyway?"

She was about to answer when he cut her off.

"No, never mind, don't tell me. Just keep it someplace safe, in case you need it."

"It is," she said.

"That's my girl. Are we okay now?"

"I guess so."

"Okay, baby, I gotta go. Be good."

She smiled. "You already know I am."

He laughed softly. "You might have to show me again."

Then the line clicked and Kate felt a glowing warmth spread through her, the kind of warmth that accompanies a deep crush, what teenage girls often mistake for love. But there was also some uncertainty there and she knew that Bree was worried about what she'd gotten herself into. She wished she could read the girl's thoughts as well, but that didn't seem to be one of the benefits of this particular parlor trick.

It was all about feelings. Emotion.

And Bree Branford had those in spades.

They sat up now and reached for the stuffed bear lying on the bed, then unzipped the battery compartment and put the phone inside. They zipped it back up, set the bear on the shelf beside the bed, then climbed off the mattress and headed for the bedroom door.

There was a mirror on the back of it and Kate caught a glimpse of Bree's worried expression. Without make-up she looked every bit the teenage girl she was. Then the door opened and they went into a dark hallway and down to the bathroom—but not the one Bree normally used. Instead they stepped inside the bigger bathroom, the one reserved for her little sisters, where Kate had frantically searched for a wash cloth back when she was a clueless cop simply trying to help a little boy in distress.

They closed the door, then opened the linen cupboard and crouched in front of it. And Kate sensed an obsessiveness about the task, a quickening of the heartbeat, that led her to believe Bree had done this many more times than she needed to.

They reached inside to the bottom shelf and pulled out a fresh roll of toilet paper. But Kate knew Bree wasn't here to replenish her supply. Looking down at the hole in the toilet roll, they stuck a fingernail into the space where the cardboard tube and the toilet paper made contact, then carefully pried it back to reveal a small piece of plastic hidden inside, about the size and shape of a postage stamp.

Kate had no trouble recognizing what it was.

A data chip.

They stared at it, the heartbeat slowing again—that sense of urgency waning—then pushed the cardboard back in place and returned the roll to the bottom shelf. The worry Bree had felt dissipated slightly, as they got to their feet and closed the cupboard doors.

As they turned to leave, the sound of the doorbell startled them. A dog started to bark and a voice from another room—a woman's voice—called out, "Thad, can you answer the door? I'm trying to get dinner ready."

"I'm on it," a voice called back.

They moved into the hallway now and back toward Bree's bedroom, the dog still barking as the indistinct murmur of voices filtered toward them from the front room. Kate heard Bree's sisters laughing in the kitchen with their mother, but she sensed no feelings of warmth in Bree. Only the cold resentment of a teenage girl living with people she had come to despise.

They had almost reached the bedroom when they heard a shout—Thad Branford calling out in surprise and anger, "What the hell are you—?"

Then his voice was abruptly cut-off by the sound of grunts and groans and furniture crashing. The heartbeat kicked up again and after a moment of hesitation, they turned and started back down the hall, a creeping sense of terror rising.

The dog was still barking and Bree's mother screamed, an agonizing, "Oh my God! OH MY GOD!!"

And now they picked up speed, running past the girls' bathroom toward the living room. One of the girls was screaming and Kate heard a grunt, followed by a loud thumping sound, and the girl immediately went quiet. Kate knew what that sound was and wanted to shout at Bree, *don't go in there, for godsakes don't go in there,* but she was only along for the ride.

They barreled down the hall, then stopped short in the door-way looking onto the living room. One of the lamps was over-turned, its bulb shattered, and Thad Branford lay on the floor in semi-darkness, blood pooling around his head, Chelsea lying near the kitchen, a dazed look in her eyes, blood trickling down her forehead, her mouth moving soundlessly.

In the center of the room, a man wearing plastic gloves and a hooded disposable coverall was hunched over the body of little Becca Branford, delivering blow after blow with a claw hammer.

Horror and disbelief exploded inside Bree. She screamed and they stumbled back against the hallway wall. Then her survival instincts kicked in, and they turned together and started to run, catching only a glimpse of the man as he got to his feet, his face little more than a blur.

They barreled back down the hallway, past the bathroom and around the corner past Bree's room and on to the mud room at the back of the house. They were about to reach the rear door when hands grabbed them by the hair and slammed them to the floor.

Kate felt pain rocketing through Bree's scalp and body as they hit the wood hard, and a gruff voice above them hissed, "This is all on you, you little skank."

Kate tried to recognize that voice but she couldn't place it, any more than she could see the man's face as the hammer began to deliver its blows, Bree turning away from him and covering her head.

The dog was in the room now, barking furiously, as the girl's terror was compounded by Kate's, the blows reigning down, dazing them, blood running into Bree's eyes, clouding her vision.

And as much as Kate wanted to see that face, she couldn't take this anymore. It was too much, too goddamn much, and she needed to be gone, to be away from here, to be out of this girl's body and back where she belonged.

The dog kept barking and Bree was crying now, shouting out for her attacker to stop, please stop and Kate shouted right along with her, "No... No... No... No..." as the blows continued.

Then the man stopped to catch his breath, the hammer hanging loosely in his hand. And Bree, barely conscious now, whimpering, finally lowered her arms and looked up at him through her blood filled eyes.

She tried to blink the blood away, and for the first time since this ordeal began, Kate saw the man's face... his features obscured, blurry... but that didn't keep her from recognizing him immediately. She recoiled inwardly, not wanting to believe what she was seeing, hoping it was a trick of the mind...

But no. It was *him* all right.

And she had no doubts that he was stone cold crazy.

As she tried to come to terms with this, with the horror of it, the room began to spin around her and she was once again sucked into the black vortex, shedding Bree's body, as a distant voice shouted "Kate! Kate!" and hands slapped her face.

Her eyes sprang open and she found herself on the floor of the Branford living room, Noah Weston hovering over her.

She batted at him, shouting, "Stay away! Keep away from me!"

And as Weston stepped away, Kate dropped the photo album, then backed into a corner and desperately tried to catch her breath.

"Are you all right?" he asked.

"Do I fucking look all right? I just got beaten half to death."

"Jesus Christ," he murmured. "Did you see the guy? Did you see who did it?"

She sucked in a deep breath and nodded.

"So is it someone you know?"

She nodded again and released the breath, not wanting to say the name out loud, because saying it out loud would make it true and she desperately didn't want it to be true.

"Well?" Weston asked. "Who is it?"

She finally relented, the words coming out in shaky gasps.

"...My old boss... ...Rusty Patterson..."

40

HE DIDN'T ANSWER UNTIL THE third ring of the bell.

The apartment was a modest third floor walk-up, not much different than Kate's, but with a view of the Pacific that put most views to shame. Right now the sea was a sparkling black diamond, quiet and nearly motionless, as if it understood the solemnity of the moment.

Rusty opened his door, looked out at Kate and feigned surprise. But he knew why she was there.

He knew.

"Hey, Kate, what's up?"

"Mind if I come inside for a minute?"

"Sure, why not," he said, then stepped back and gestured. "Come on in."

She moved past him into his living room and reacquainted herself with its furnishings. In all the years she worked with Rusty she had only been to his apartment half a dozen times.

"In case you're wondering, MacLean and Linkenfeld are downstairs and they've got a couple of unis with them. I figured since you're the reason I've got this job, the least I could do is give you a moment alone, give you a chance to talk about it."

He frowned, giving it a valiant effort, but the words sounded hollow. "Talk about what? What's going on?"

Kate brought her arm out from behind her back and offered him the roll of toilet paper she'd found. "You forgot something at the Branford house."

He looked puzzled. "What?"

"You left it, and a bunch like it, scattered on the bathroom floor when you ransacked the place. You looked right past it, just like we did, and you gotta hand it to Bree. Her clever little hiding places almost kept you from being caught."

She showed him the hidden data chip and he looked at it, then at her, and he didn't disappoint her by carrying on the charade.

His shoulders slumped and he crossed to the sofa and sat. It was only then that she noticed something he apparently hadn't: a small patch of blood seeping through his shirt near his left ribs. One of her bullets had caught him after all.

"So I guess I should call my lawyer?" he said.

"You can, but I don't know how much good it'll do you. We've watched the videos and the girl in them is clearly Bree Branford, and she's clearly underage, and you clearly violated her in a number of different ways."

"Doesn't mean I murdered her and her family."

"Believe me, I wish it didn't. And I suppose you could try to convince a jury that one plus one doesn't necessarily equal two, but once they get a look at the videos, they'll be lost to you forever."

"It's not like I was diddling a five-year-old boy. She wasn't a child, Kate. She was sixteen years old."

"That *is* a child. You know that as well as I do."

"Who cares how old she was? Look what she did for a living. She was a common skank and she probably would've been dead from disease or drugs before her twentieth birthday."

Kate was appalled. "So she deserves to have her skull smashed in with a hammer?"

He studied her for a long moment, then lowered his gaze, and stared at the floor.

"I didn't mean for any of that to happen. Not like that. Believe me, I didn't know that was a side of me that even existed, but the Sorianos were pressuring me, and then I found out who the girl really was, and that her parents were no better. I thought maybe they were involved in it, too, and that's when the rage came." He looked up at her again. "I couldn't control it, Kate. I tried, but I couldn't stop myself."

"I don't get it," she said. "What went wrong?"

"That's just it. I don't *know*. It's just like my old partner, the one I told you about, the one who raped that nurse before he put a bullet in his brain."

"Fuck you, Rusty. Don't blame this on the job."

"What else do I blame it on? You think I like what I am? You think I *wanted* to be this... this... beast?"

The choice of words sent something cold and clammy skittering up Kate's spine. She thought about him grunting and groaning as he swung that hammer, the stink of the sweat, and the blood... and the word *beast* was certainly the most accurate description of what she'd seen and heard.

She thought about Christopher's words...

There's more than one kind of beast out there, and we should always do what we can to stop them.

She took her phone out and dialed and when MacLean answered, she said, "We're on our way down." Then she clicked off and took her cuffs out and gestured. "Stand up, Rusty. I need to read you your rights."

She half expected him to try to make a move, to pull out a piece he had hidden somewhere in the sofa and give this saga the dramatic—if clichéd—ending it called out for.

But that wasn't Rusty Patterson. He was the PR guy. The man who got along with everyone. The man who was always smoothing the waters when things started to get rough.

Except, of course, when he was bashing people's heads in.

41

THE FOLLOWING MORNING, AS THEY stood outside their motel room, Christopher tried to convince Kate to go with them.

They had never really unpacked, so, for them, it was a simple matter of throwing their things in the Rambler and once again hitting the road. But for Kate it would have meant uprooting her entire life, such as it was, and leaving behind the town she had grown up in.

Weston didn't seem to share Chris's desire, but it wouldn't have mattered if he had.

"I can't just drop everything and go, Chris. I've got my father to think about, and my job. And they'll be putting Rusty on trial in a few months and I'll have to be here for that."

What about the other policemen? Can't they do it?

"They could, but I'm the lead on the case and that means I should be the one to testify."

But I came here for you. I came here because she wanted me to. She wanted me to find you.

This was the first time Chris had sounded his age, and it broke her heart.

"I know," she said. "And you *did* find me. And look what we did together. We've stopped a very bad man from ever hurting anyone again."

But he's not the only one she wants you to stop, Kate. You know that.

"Yes, but I can't do what you and Noah do. I can't go through what I did last night. Not again. It takes too much out of me."

Then we'll find a way to control it. To make it easier for you.

"Somehow I think it controls us more than we'll ever be able to control it. Whatever *it* is."

We'll find a way. I promise.

She shook her head. "No, Chris. I think what you need to do is stop chasing around the country and find a family. A good family. One that can take care of you."

Noah takes care of me. And you could, too.

He started to cry and she pulled him into her arms and if her heart was breaking before, she thought it might now be irrevocably fractured, because this odd boy had managed to touch her in just the few hours they'd been together, and she knew she would spend many a night wondering if she had made the wrong decision.

But no. This was where she belonged.

When Chris was done crying, he pulled away from her, went to the Rambler and leaned toward the back seat. He came back carrying his pink photo album and held it out to her.

I want you to have this.

Kate stared at it. Hesitated.

It's okay. There's nothing to see now. I just want you to have it to remember me by.

Now tears filled *Kate's* eyes and she hugged him again and took the album from his hands as he gave her one last squeeze, then climbed into the back seat.

Weston closed him inside.

"For what it's worth," he said, "you may be a pain in the ass sometimes, but I wouldn't object if you changed your mind."

"Are you sure about that?"

He shrugged. "No. But I figured it was the polite thing to say."

She smiled. "You know, that forty-eight hours isn't up. You keep talking like that and I may have to reconsider letting you two go."

He returned the smile. "I'm afraid you'd have to catch us, first."

Then he got in the car, started the engine, and drove away.

EPILOGUE

"Every new beginning comes from some other beginning's end."

~Seneca

42

TWO WEEKS LATER, KATE'S FATHER died.

She had come over for her usual Wednesday night to find him sitting in his chair, his oxygen tank hissing, his eyes closed, his body still.

No last words had been spoken. No regrets expressed.

Not to Kate, anyway.

He looked peaceful, and she was glad for that, but true to their history she felt no real pain at his passing. Just the usual touch of guilt for her failure to love a man who was never really capable of loving anyone.

In the days that followed, Kate found that she'd begun to distance herself from the job—a job she had worked so hard to obtain. In the wake of the revelations of Rusty Patterson's savagery, the legitimacy of the position was tainted, as was the entire department.

They all felt it. All wanted to wish it away. But none more than Kate herself.

And she just didn't feel the passion anymore. She woke up every morning feeling listless and alone and, worst of all, without any sense of purpose.

There was talk that she was about to be demoted, but she honestly didn't care.

·

The day after Rusty's arrest, Kate got a call from Stokes County ADA Charles Dillman.

"You never got back to me," he said. "How did your interview with the kid go?"

"Nowhere. That was all a dead end that had nothing to do with my case, so I cut them loose."

"You what?"

"We had no evidence of molestation, and no reason to hold Weston."

"Do you have any idea where they went?"

"Not a clue."

"Christ," Dillman said.

"I know you're invested in this guy's guilt," Kate told him, "but I think you've got it wrong. He doesn't strike me as a killer."

"Oh, really? Then you want to explain what he and that boy were doing up in Tacoma near that crime scene you told me about?"

"You know that for a fact?"

"Not a hundred percent, but one of the detectives I spoke to says he saw a guy with an odd-looking kid parked down the street from the murder house in an old beat-up Rambler station wagon. Is that what they were driving?"

Kate didn't hesitate. "No. They're traveling by train."

"You sure about that? Because I gotta tell you, I've got an itch when it comes to this fella, and I hope I'm not being lied to by a sworn police officer."

"That's a pretty bold accusation. Why would I lie?"

"I don't know," he said. "You tell me."

Kate sighed. "I don't have time for this, Mr. Dillman. So why don't you save the aggressive bullshit for the courtroom and let me get back to work."

Before he could respond, she hung up on him.

•

In the days that followed, Kate often thought about Christopher, and even Weston, and wondered where they might be. What part of the country had they traveled to? What kind of trouble were they getting themselves into?

One night, after several glasses of wine, she lit some candles, drew a bath, and spent the good part of an hour in the tub, trying to soak away the regret she had begun to feel for staying behind. She was toweling off and headed into her bedroom, which she had also adorned with candles, and a glint of light in her dresser mirror caught her attention.

It was the pink plastic cover of the photo album Christopher had left behind.

She thought she had put it in a drawer, but there it was, sitting atop her dresser as if it were waiting for her to pick it up.

She paused uneasily, as she always did when she saw it, but then stepped over and took it in her hands, staring down at the name written there with a bright blue marker:

Lucy.

It suddenly occurred to her that she had never asked Christopher who Lucy was. She remembered opening the book in her office that first time before she was whisked away, and seeing several photographs of a little girl. A girl she thought might be Lucy.

Now she opened it again, expecting to see that canned family portrait, but to her surprise the photos of the girl had returned, and she flipped through them one by one, taking the time to study them more carefully.

She was a cute little girl with a wonderful smile, who obviously had down syndrome. And judging by the children who surrounded her in several of the photographs, she was a resident of the group home Christopher had once lived in. The place where he'd been attacked by the Beast.

Where they had *all* been attacked.

But it was the very last photograph that tugged at Kate's heart. It was a picture of the same girl, standing together with Christopher, the two holding hands. And as she stared at it, she knew she could be imagining things, but she thought she saw it.... *move.*

Then, she felt a faint tingling in her skull as Christopher's melodic voice came to her like a distant radio transmission:

He didn't kill us all, Kate.

She's alive. Lucy's alive.

And the Beast took her with him.

•

Less than twenty-four hours later, Kate finished packing, climbed behind the wheel of her SUV and drove toward the sound of Christopher's voice.

We hope you enjoyed this book, and if you did, we'd greatly appreciate a quick review on Amazon, Goodreads and other review sites. And be sure to tell your friends about the book as well.

Authors and publishing houses live and die by our readers, and reviews go a long way toward spreading the word about a good book.

If you have any questions about the Linger Series or any of our other books, feel free to contact us at *BraunHausMedia.com*

Thank you.

Robert Gregory-Browne
Editorial Director

Made in the USA
Middletown, DE
21 February 2021

34136256R00116